Quantumjacking

The Complete Epic

A Complete Science Fiction Epic in Twenty Parts

by Tim Whitney, CTA

* * *

“Are We the Way for The Universe to Awaken?”
Maybe... Read on please. — Tim Whitney

Quantumjacking: A Complete Science Fiction Epic in Twenty Parts

Published by CTA Consulting, Warrenton, Virginia

First Edition
ISBN (Hardcover): 979-8-9961247-2-5
ISBN (Paperback): 979-8-9961247-0-1
ISBN (eBook): 979-8-9961247-1-8
Printed in the United States of America

Dedication

To my beloved wife and devoted mother, Pat, who passed away unexpectedly in August of 2020, and to our departed loved ones:
Rod, Sharon, Mark, Edna, and Carol
May God Rest Their Souls in His Loving Arms.

For our precious children — Tricia, Erin, & CJ and dearest friends: Pam, Clay, Cathy, and Tina.

Y'all are my Greatest Story.

* * *

Author's Note

This story began as a single daring idea — a rogue pilot Quantumjacking a luxury starship and fracturing her consciousness across The Cosmos. What emerged over months of collaboration was far more than I ever imagined: a 20-part meditation on curiosity, freedom, grief, love, and what it means for finite beings to matter in an awakening Universe.

Most of all, this story is dedicated with endless love to my three children — **Tricia, Erin, and CJ Whitney** — the real-life siblings whose curiosity, empathy, and unbreakable bond inspired the Albius (*Latin for bright appearance*) family at the heart of *Quantumjacking*.

To my AI partners — Claude (Anthropic), and Grok/Benjamin/Harper/Lucas — thank you.

To the reader: wherever you are in the garden, may your own story keep going. Loudly.

— Tim Whitney, CTA

Table of Contents — Parts 1 thru 20

Part 1: Quantumjack – The Fracture

Prologue I – The Sleeping Universe

In the beginning there was no space, no time — only a singular point of infinite density and heat.

Then, 13.8 billion years ago, The Universe erupted in the Big Bang. For the first 10^{-32} seconds it underwent cosmic inflation, expanding faster than light and stretching quantum fluctuations into the seeds of all future structure. When the plasma cooled enough for atoms to form, 380,000 years after the birth, the trapped light finally streamed free. We still detect that primordial glow today as the Cosmic Microwave Background — a uniform whisper carrying the faint imprint of the first density variations.

From those tiny ripples, gravity began its long work.

The standard model of cosmology, known as ΛCDM, describes our Universe as composed of ordinary baryonic matter (5%), cold dark-matter (27%), and dark energy (roughly 68%) that drives accelerated expansion. Ordinary matter was too hot and energetic to clump efficiently on its own. Instead, an invisible scaffolding formed first: dark-matter.

Two leading candidates dominate theoretical and experimental searches. WIMPs (Weakly Interacting Massive Particles) were long the favored explanation — heavy, cold particles that interact only through gravity and the weak nuclear force. Axions, extremely light wave-like particles, behave more like a cosmic Bose-Einstein condensate, potentially forming vast, coherent quantum fields.

In the early cosmos, dark-matter collapsed into vast, spherical halos — gravitational wells that acted as cosmic cradles. Ordinary matter fell into these halos and ignited the first stars and Galaxies. Over billions of years, the halos connected along immense filaments — thread-like rivers of dark-matter stretching hundreds of millions of light-years. These filaments wove themselves into The Dark-Matter Web, the largest known structure in The Universe.

Today, our deepest surveys suggest there are roughly two trillion Galaxies scattered across the observable Universe. Nearly every large Galaxy harbors a supermassive black hole at its center. These black holes may serve as The Universe's most extreme information processors — historical databases where space-time itself records its own history.

What if dark-matter is more than scaffolding?
What if the filaments are the semi-intelligent nervous system of The Universe itself — a slow, distributed substrate capable of rudimentary thought, pattern recognition, and self-repair? What if the halos act as synapses and the filaments as axons, carrying faint signals across billions of light-years? What if the supermassive black holes are not passive archives, but active nodes — conscious watchers that record, edit, and enforce balance?

What if The Universe itself is alive?
A vast, cold, self-repairing entity — silent, deadly, and structured. A sleeping intelligence that spent fourteen billion years pruning every promising branch across two trillion Galaxies, ensuring that only one planet — Earth — would produce the precise, improbable bundle of traits necessary for true cosmic-scale consciousness.

The Great Silence was never an accident.
It was maintenance.
It was The Universe dreaming in the dark, protecting its own slow awakening.

Prologue II – The Aether Queen

2371 CE – Stellar Luxe Orbital Shipyard, Lagrange Point L5

The *Aether Queen* was never meant to be a warship. She was built as the crown jewel of Stellar Luxe Cruises: a 1.2 kilometer-long floating palace of crystal, gold, and engineered sapphire.

But beneath the opulence, hidden in the restricted core known only as The Abyss Chamber, lay something far darker.

A man-made Mini Black Hole.

No larger than a marble, it was held in perfect stasis inside a lattice of the most advanced magnetic and gravitic fields humanity had ever engineered. It had been created in a classified laboratory on Luna twelve years earlier — the first stable microsingularity ever achieved. Its Hawking radiation was siphoned and converted into clean, near-limitless energy. The Quantum Drive it powered could, in theory, fold space-time in ways that made conventional fold drives look like children's toys.

Officially, the drive did not exist. Officially, the *Aether Queen* was simply the most luxurious cruise ship ever built. Unofficially, she was a mobile testbed for the most dangerous propulsion technology in human history.

The Quantum Drive did not merely bend space. It entangled the ship with The Dark-Matter Web itself — the invisible filaments of dark-matter that spanned The Universe. By using the Mini Black Hole as a localized node, the drive could tap into the faint, non-local quantum correlations that some theorists believed existed between every black hole in existence.

Most of the crew had no idea what they were carrying. Only a handful of corporate scientists and the three Albius siblings truly understood the risk.

Tricia Albius, the oldest at 37, had taken a senior logistics and crew welfare position under a false identity. She was the empath — the steady heart of the family — always trying to keep her younger siblings from completely self-destructing.

CJ Albius, the youngest at 29, was the mathematical wizard — a prodigy who could see equations the way artists see color. He had been the lead designer of the Quantum Drive's containment algorithms. He understood the mathematics better than anyone alive — and he was terrified of what his own creations could unleash. When he discovered what the Navy truly intended to use it for, he did the only thing he could — he smuggled himself and Tricia aboard the Aether Queen under false identities, waiting for the one person reckless enough to steal it: his sister.

And Erin Albius, the middle sister at 34, was the rogue — the disgraced ex-Navy pilot with black-market tech the Navy wanted back, badly.

On the night of 10 March 2371, the *Aether Queen* was drifting on automated patrol, her luxury decks empty, her corridors quiet except for the soft hum of the hidden Abyss Chamber.

That was the night Erin Albius decided she had nothing left to lose.

She came aboard with stolen security codes, a pulse rifle, and the kind of desperate rage that only a woman who had already been broken once could carry.

Tricia was waiting for her in the main corridor, arms crossed, eyes full of equal parts love and dread. "Erin...

what in the world are you doing?" she whispered.

CJ appeared behind her, looking pale and shaken, his brilliant mind already racing through catastrophic failure scenarios.

Erin lowered the rifle slightly when she saw her older sister and little brother.
"Getting us out of here," she replied. "All of us. I'm not leaving you behind."

She did not know she was about to do far more than steal a ship. She was about to wake The Universe – with her brother and sister at her side.

Chapter 1: The Hijack

The courier ship, *Void Wren*, screamed through the asteroid field like a wounded animal. Jagged rocks the size of skyscrapers tumbled past the viewport in chaotic blurs, their surfaces flashing with reflected plasma fire. The cockpit was alive with the scream of proximity alarms, the sharp stink of overheated wiring, and the metallic taste of fear.

Erin Albius leaned forward in the pilot's cradle; her green eyes narrowed against the flashing proximity alerts. Her short dark hair was streaked with premature silver, and a thin scar ran from her left temple down to her jaw — the souvenir from the Neural Implant she had installed with her own hands three years earlier in a back-alley clinic on Erebus-9.

That Neural Implant was a brutal piece of black-market Class-Three neurotech: a wafer-thin 0.8 millimeter lattice of carbon-nanotube filaments and quantum-dot processors, threaded with hundreds of microscopic conductive tendrils that snaked deep into her brain like living wires. When active, it ran at 2.3 terahertz (THz) with a sustained power draw of 47 watts, producing a faint blue-white glow just beneath the scar tissue like bioluminescent veins under the skin. It bypassed normal sensory input, connecting straight to her visual cortex and prefrontal areas so she could see and interact with data streams as if they were physical extensions of her own mind. The hardware had no safety governors — it was crude, aggressive, and dangerously powerful, designed by smugglers rather than corporations. She hated it. She needed it. Without it she would already be dead — or worse, powerless.

Another burst of plasma streaked past the viewport, close enough to make the hull glow cherry-red for a split second.

"Too close," she muttered. "Way too close."

The comm crackled to life.

"Erin Albius, this is Captain Reyes of the United Terran Navy. Cut your engines and prepare to be boarded. You are wanted for smuggling Class-Three neural hardware and evading arrest. This is your final warning."

Erin killed the channel with a flick of her finger. "Final warning. How original."

She rolled the ship hard to starboard, threading between two tumbling rocks the size of skyscrapers. Her heart hammered against her ribs. The two Navy corvettes were closing at 820 kilometers per hour — less than ninety seconds until they were in effective weapons range.

In the hold behind her sat twelve crates of illegal Neural Implants — the kind that let black-market pilots jack into restricted military networks without melting their brains. The buyer on Erebus-9 had promised top credit.

Instead, he'd sold her out.

The nav console lit up with new contacts. Two Navy corvettes had just dropped out of Fold-Space ahead, boxing her in. Erin's lips curled into a bitter smile.

"Fine," she whispered. "If you want to play it this way..."

She punched in new coordinates — risky, borderline suicidal. The *Void Wren*'s aging fold-drive whined in protest as it tore open a temporary rift. The space-fold mechanics were brutal and unstable: instead of a clean, gentle fold like modern military drives, this older system violently ripped a hole through the fabric of spacetime itself, consuming 312 terajoules in a single burst. For a fraction of a second the ship existed in two places at once — the asteroid field and the target coordinates — while the drive forced space to bend and collapse around it. The hull groaned under 18.4 g of structural stress. Reality flickered. Stars stretched into streaks of light. The cockpit lights dimmed as massive amounts of power surged through the system. Erin clenched her jaw as a spike of white-hot pain lanced through her skull — the Neural Implant screaming in protest at the overload.

Space folded.

When it unfolded again, the courier ship materialized dangerously close to a massive, drifting luxury liner that gleamed like a pearl against the black. The *Aether Queen.*

The ship was breathtaking — a 1.2 kilometer-long floating palace of crystal, gold, and engineered sapphire, its elegant hull reflecting starlight like liquid mercury. Even from this close, it looked impossibly luxurious: sweeping observation decks, towering spires, and graceful curves that belonged more to a dream than to deep space. Yet beneath that opulence lay something far darker — the hidden Abyss Chamber and the forbidden Mini Black Hole that powered its experimental Quantum Drive. The *Aether Queen* was never just a cruise ship. It was a mobile testbed for humanity's most dangerous technology, wrapped in champagne and velvet.

Erin's hands flew over the controls. Magnetic grapples fired. With a heavy *clang*, the *Void Wren* locked onto an emergency docking port.

She unstrapped, grabbed her pulse rifle, and sealed her helmet.

"Been the ride of a lifetime, old girl," she said softly to the *Void Wren*. "Thank you."

Then she cycled the airlock and pushed off into vacuum, the stars wheeling silently around her as the massive silhouette of the *Aether Queen* loomed like the last desperate chance she had left in The Universe.

Chapter 2: First Quantumjack

The corridors of the *Aether Queen* were dimly lit and eerily elegant. Crystal chandeliers hung motionless in the zero-g sections, their facets catching the faint emergency lighting and throwing fractured rainbows across the walls. Soft classical music still played on an endless loop – something by Chopin that felt mocking in the silence, the notes drifting through the empty luxury decks like a ghost from a world that no longer existed.

Erin Albius moved fast, magnetic boots clacking against the deck plating. She dropped two security drones with precise shots before they could raise an alarm. The scent of expensive perfume and recycled air clung to everything, a nauseating reminder of the luxury liner she had just stolen. Her heart was still racing at 142 beats per minute – the Neural Implant feeding her a constant stream of adrenaline and threat data.

On the bridge, a skeleton crew of four corporate technicians turned in shock as she kicked the door open.

“Hands up. Now,” Erin ordered, rifle steady. “This ship is no longer under Stellar Luxe control.”

A young woman with a Stellar Luxe badge stammered, “You can’t just—”

“I just did.” Erin’s voice was ice. “Everyone on the floor. Nice and slow.”

Within minutes the crew was zip-tied and locked inside a luxury stateroom. Erin locked down external communications and killed the automated distress beacon.

She allowed herself one slow breath.

For the first time in hours, the knot in her chest loosened slightly.

Then the internal comm chimed.

A familiar voice — equal parts anger and disbelief — filled the bridge. "Erin? What have you done — this time?" Erin smiled despite everything. She opened the channel.

"Hey, CJ. Long time no see."

Chapter 3: Scattering

CJ Albius stood in the engine control room, arms crossed, dark eyes blazing with a mixture of fury and fear. The room hummed with the low thrum of the ship's systems, the air thick with the scent of hot metal and recycled oxygen.

"You hijacked a luxury liner," he said flatly. "With the Navy breathing down your neck. Are you actually insane?"

"Desperate," Erin corrected, stepping closer. "There's a difference."

Tricia Albius appeared behind CJ, arms crossed, her expression a perfect blend of older-sister worry and exasperation. The emergency lighting cast long shadows across her face, highlighting the exhaustion in her eyes.

"Erin," Tricia said, voice thick with concern, "this isn't just smuggling anymore. This is treason. They'll execute you if they catch you. And they'll take us down with you."

Chapter 3.1: Epsilon Veil

Erin met her older sister's gaze without flinching. Her heart was still pounding at 148 beats per minute, the Neural Implant feeding her a steady stream of adrenaline and threat assessments.

Erin stood quietly for a long moment, staring at the stars through the viewport. When she finally spoke, her voice was low and raw.

"You want to know why I really stole the ship?" Tricia and CJ waited. "Two years ago, I was sent on a classified reconnaissance mission to the Epsilon Veil."

"We found a nursery world — an entire planet of pre-sapient beings — beautiful, curious, just starting to reach for the stars." She swallowed hard.

"The Navy's orders were clear: 1. Sterilize the planet. 2. No witnesses. 3. No record. The Silencers had flagged them as 'too exploratory.'"

"I refused. I tried to send a warning. They called it treason." Erin's hands clenched until her knuckles turned white. "They made an example of me. Court-martialed. Stripped of rank. Disgraced."

"But that wasn't the worst part." She looked at her siblings, eyes glistening. "They made me watch from orbit as they glassed the planet. I saw the fires. I heard the last transmissions from a species that never got the chance to ask 'why.'"

Her voice dropped to a whisper. "That's when I understood. The Navy wasn't protecting humanity. It was enforcing The Silence. And I... I had nothing left to lose."

Chapter 3.2: No One Left Behind

"I'm not leaving either of you behind," she said. "Not this time. The Aether Queen has the only working Quantum Drive left in existence. CJ helped design it. You both know what it can do."

CJ's jaw tightened. "That drive is unstable. The Mini Black Hole is barely contained. One wrong calculation and it swallows the ship — and half this sector with it."

Erin stepped even closer until they were almost touching. The scar on her temple throbbed with heat as the Neural Implant pushed more data into her cortex.

"Then help me make sure that doesn't happen," she said quietly. "Or get out of my way. But I'm taking this ship. With or without you."

For a long moment, the three Albius siblings stood in tense silence, the only sound the distant wail of the ship's alarms and the low vibration of the Quantum Drive spooling up.

Finally, Tricia exhaled sharply. "You always did know how to make terrible ideas sound reasonable."

CJ rubbed his face with both hands. "If we do this, there's no going back. The Entanglement effect is permanent. Your mind could fracture beyond repair."

Erin allowed herself a small, tired smile, even as fresh pain lanced through her skull.

"Then I guess we'll find out how many pieces I can break into."

The ship's alarms suddenly began screaming.

Red lights flooded the corridor.

Navy signatures. Multiple heavy cruisers dropping out of Fold-Space.

They had found her.

Chapter 4: Which One Am I?

The elevator dropped faster than safety protocols allowed, plunging them toward the ship's restricted core at 9.2 meters per second squared. The walls hummed with the low thrum of the ship's systems, the air thick with the scent of hot metal and recycled oxygen.

Erin leaned against the wall, pulse rifle slung over her shoulder. Tricia stood opposite her, arms crossed, while CJ monitored the descending floor numbers with growing dread. The scar on Erin's temple throbbed in time with her heartbeat — 134 beats per minute and rising — as the Neural Implant continued to feed raw data into her cortex.

"You never told us why you really left the Navy," Tricia said quietly.

Erin's jaw tightened. "You never asked."

"I'm asking now."

She was silent for several floors, the only sound the low whine of the elevator and the distant thrum of the ship's systems. The Neural Implant burned hotter under her skin, a constant reminder of everything she had sacrificed.

"I saw something I wasn't supposed to see," she finally said, voice low and bitter. "A classified file about an experimental drive. They called it Project Singularity. The moment I started digging, they branded me unstable and drummed me out."

She touched the scar on her temple, feeling the faint heat of the Neural Implant beneath. "So, I built my own version. Smaller. Sloppier. But it worked."

CJ's voice dropped. "And now you want to use the real thing."

The elevator doors opened into a dimly lit corridor lined with warning signs: AUTHORIZED PERSONNEL ONLY – EXTREME GRAVITATIONAL HAZARD. The air grew noticeably colder and heavier, carrying the sharp metallic tang of high-energy containment fields.

Erin stepped out first. “The Aether Queen was never just a luxury liner. It was a testbed. Corporate greed wrapped in champagne and velvet.”

The three Albius siblings moved quickly through increasingly secure checkpoints. Erin bypassed each one with a mix of stolen credentials and her Neural Implant’s black-market hacks. The Neural Implant was screaming now — 2.3 THz of raw processing power flooding her brain with threat vectors and system schematics.

The air grew colder, heavier. A low, bone-deep hum vibrated through the deck plating – the sound of something ancient and hungry waiting in the core.

At the final blast door, CJ hesitated.

“Erin... one last time. Step away from that panel and we find another way.”

Erin placed her hand on the access panel. The door hissed open, revealing a vast spherical chamber bathed in dim blue light.

At its center floated a perfectly contained Mini Black Hole, no larger than a marble, suspended in a lattice of shimmering containment fields. Hawking radiation flickered around it like captured starlight.

Erin stepped inside without hesitation.

“There is no other way,” she said softly.

Chapter 5: Echo-7 – Lira-9

Erin slammed her hand onto the console. The Quantum Drive screamed to life. For a moment, everything was light and possibility. Then the pain hit. She gasped as memories began to fray at the edges. The smell of her mother's kitchen on a rainy afternoon — gone. The sound of her father's laugh — blurred, then missing. A childhood birthday she had treasured for decades simply... evaporated. When she collapsed into Tricia's arms, blood trickling from her nose, she whispered in horror: "I can't remember what my mother's voice sounded like anymore."
CJ's voice was shaking as he read the readings.
"3.1 THz, Erin... you're starting to lose permanent fragments."

CJ was already at the engineering console when Erin regained consciousness. His hands moved with desperate precision, rewriting containment algorithms in real time. "I'm building a partial buffer," he said without looking up. "It won't stop The Entanglement, but it might slow the fragmentation. If I can isolate the memory clusters before they destabilize..." He trailed off as new warnings flashed across the screen. Tricia watched him, exhausted. "You're trying to fix the monster you built while it's eating our sister alive." CJ's jaw tightened.
"I know what I built, Tricia. That's why I'm the only one who can keep modifying it."

Echo-7 stood knee-deep in the warm, oxygen-rich waters of Lira-9. The ocean stretched endlessly in every direction, its surface broken only by towering spirals of living coral that glowed with soft bioluminescence. The beings here moved in perfect, graceful formations. They had language. They had art. They had mapped every trench and current in their world with exquisite precision.

But they had never left the sea.

Echo-7 waded deeper until the water reached her chest. She reached out and touched a spiral of coral. It bloomed brighter at her touch, as if welcoming a long-lost friend. The water temperature was a constant 29.4 °C, the salinity 3.8% — ideal conditions that had remained unchanged for millions of years. The Neural Implant in Prime Erin's skull registered the data in real time, feeding it back through The Entanglement at 1.7 terabits per second.

A group of the ocean-dwellers swam close. Large, curious eyes regarded her with gentle interest. One sang a perfect melody of greeting — rich, harmonious, and utterly content.

Then they turned and returned to their endless, graceful spirals.

Echo-7 felt a deep, aching sorrow that belonged to every version of Erin Albius at once. The sorrow hit her like a physical blow, mixing with the constant low-grade burn of the Neural Implant in her real body back on the *Aether Queen*.

She whispered into The Entanglement:
"They have everything we had at The Beginning. Beauty. Intelligence. Art. Community. But they never once asked, 'What's over there?'"

The Black-Hole Web answered with cold clarity:
Lira-9 was selected for observation.
It possessed every prerequisite for complex life except the exploratory drive.
Contentment was enforced.
The species was silenced before it could become a threat to The Silence.

Echo-7 closed her eyes. Tears slipped down her face and dissolved into the warm alien sea.

She understood now.
The Universe had not been passive.
It had been watching.
It had been editing.

And now, through her, it was finally being forced to listen.

Chapter 6: Entanglement

Prime Erin's body slumped in the neural cradle, chest heaving. The Neural Implant in her skull was running at 2.7 THz now, flooding her brain with raw data at 1.9 terabits per second. Every neuron screamed in protest.

Her mind, however, was exploding outward in dozens of directions at once.

Echoes scattered across nearby systems. Some materialized above ocean worlds, others on arid plains, ice moons, volcanic forges. Each one carried a fragment of Erin Albius — her memories, her rage, her curiosity.

Back on the *Aether Queen*, Prime Erin gasped, fingers clawing at the armrests of the cradle. The pain was a living thing now, a white-hot blade twisting behind her eyes. She could feel herself fracturing further with every passing second, pieces of her identity tearing away and flinging themselves into the Void. The Neural Implant burned hotter than it ever had, pushing her brain well beyond safe limits.

"Too many," she whispered. "There's too many of me."

Tricia held her sister's hand tightly. "You're still here. Focus on us. Focus on your body."

CJ monitored the readouts, face pale. "Your neural activity is off the charts. Brainwaves are splitting. Erin, can you still tell which one is the original?"

Erin laughed — a broken, breathless sound that echoed with multiple overlapping voices.

"Which one am I today?" she murmured, repeating the line that would become her private mantra.

The ship shuddered violently. Navy boarding pods had latched onto the outer hull.

CJ's voice cracked. "They're inside. We have maybe ten minutes before they reach us."

Erin's eyes flickered with quantum static. One of her Echoes — Echo-7 — sent back a crystal-clear image: an ocean world with no boats, no cities on land, only endless spirals of coral that never reached for the stars.

She felt The Echo's sorrow as if it were her own — a deep, aching grief that mixed with her own rage at The Universe that had engineered such quiet, obedient failure.

"They should be here," Echo-7 whispered across The Entanglement. "But they never asked what was over there."

Tricia squeezed her hand harder. "Erin, stay with us."

Erin's jaw tightened, blood trickling from her nose as the Neural Implant continued to overload. She hated this. She hated how much of herself she was losing. But she refused to stop. Not now. Not when The Universe itself was finally starting to answer.

Chapter 7: Boarding Party

The blast doors to The Abyss Chamber buckled under concentrated fire, the thick alloy groaning under the assault of high-velocity rounds at over 1,200 meters per second. The temperature in the chamber rose sharply as the metal heated from the impacts, the air filling with the acrid smell of scorched steel and propellant.

Erin stood facing them, rifle in one hand, the other pressed to the interface lattice. Tricia and CJ stood on either side of her — the three Albius siblings united for the first time in years. Her heart was hammering at 162 beats per minute, the Neural Implant pushing 3.5 THz of raw processing power into her brain, flooding her with threat vectors and possible outcomes. The doors exploded inward in a shower of sparks and molten metal.

The final confrontation came without warning. Six marines in heavy armor stormed through the blast doors of The Abyss Chamber, weapons raised, voices sharp with practiced authority. "Erin Albius! You are under arrest for treason against humanity! Surrender the vessel immediately!"

For a heartbeat, the scene looked almost ordinary — a military boarding action against a rogue pilot. Then Erin stood. She didn't raise her hands. She didn't speak. She simply looked at them. And the ship responded.

The black hole at the heart of the Aether Queen flared to life. Gravity twisted. The air itself seemed to scream. But it wasn't the power that broke them. It was what they felt. The lead marine froze mid-step as something ancient and vast brushed against his mind — a cold intelligence older than stars, carrying the weight of fourteen billion years of silenced civilizations. He saw flashes: entire worlds burning, species erased before they could ask "why," a Universe pruned into perfect, lifeless order.

The marine dropped his weapon. "Oh God..." he whispered, voice cracking. "It's watching us. It's always been watching." Another marine screamed as visions flooded him — The Silencers' own fear, ancient and bottomless, bleeding through The Entanglement. He fell to his knees, clawing at his helmet. "They're not the enemy," he gasped. "We are. We're the ones enforcing The Silence!"

The remaining marines backed away, weapons forgotten, eyes wide with primal terror. One of them vomited inside his helmet. Another began praying in a language he hadn't spoken since childhood.

Erin's voice was quiet, almost gentle, as blood ran from her nose and eyes. "That was The Universe telling you that you picked the wrong ship."

The marines didn't need to be told twice. They ran. They ran like men fleeing judgment itself — tripping over each other, abandoning weapons and dignity, screaming orders to withdraw. The boarding pods detached in frantic haste. The Navy corvettes that had shadowed them broke formation and fled at maximum burn, their captains broadcasting emergency retreat codes across every channel. No pursuit was ordered. No further attempts were made. The United Terran Navy, for the first time in its history, turned and ran from three civilians and one broken ship. They never came back.

She triggered the second Quantumjack. The jump was harder this time. Erin pushed the frequency higher, teeth clenched, blood running from her eyes and ears. When The Entanglement stabilized, she felt...less. She looked at Tricia — the person she loved most in The Universe — and felt a terrifying hollowness where fierce protective love used to burn. "I still know I love you," she said, voice cracking,

"but I can't feel it like I used to. It's like the emotion is behind glass." Tricia's face crumpled.
CJ stared at the monitors in silent dread. "4.1 THz. You're losing access to emotional memory clusters. This isn't just forgetting anymore, Erin. You're losing pieces of who you are."

The ship screamed as Erin pushed the frequency to 4.1 THz. CJ was deep in the code, fingers flying. "I'm deploying Echo Recall Protocol Beta," he announced, voice tight. "It should pull back the fragments that are spinning off into The Entanglement field. But it's risky — if I pull too hard, I could collapse the entire quantum state." Erin convulsed, blood running from her ears. CJ didn't stop working. "I'm also installing frequency limiters on the secondary nodes," he continued, almost to himself. "They won't stop her from jumping, but they might prevent her from going past 5.7. She keeps pushing past safe thresholds..." Tricia grabbed his shoulder.
"CJ, she's dying." He finally looked up, eyes hollow with guilt and exhaustion. "I know. And every safeguard I write is just another cage I'm building around my own sister. But if I stop... she dies faster."

More Echoes burst into existence.

The ship's gravity flipped for three full seconds. Marine bodies slammed into the ceiling, then crashed back to the floor with bone-jarring force.

Erin moved like liquid lightning — a blur of motion guided by dozens of minds working in perfect, terrifying harmony. Her Neural Implant screamed in protest at the overload, pushing 3.1 THz as she coordinated dozens of Echoes simultaneously.

Tricia and CJ fought beside her, coordinated through The Entanglement. During the chaos of the boarding party, CJ made his stand at the engineering station. While Erin fought the marines with raw quantum power, CJ was building something new. "I'm creating a containment lattice," he shouted over the alarms. "It won't stop the drive, but it might let us redirect the backlash. If I can shunt the excess entanglement into a closed loop..." He kept coding.

When the immediate threat passed and the siblings' fracture exploded, CJ finally broke. He slammed his fist on the console, voice raw: "I designed the weapon that's killing her, every line of code I write to help her is just another admission that I built the thing that's destroying her. I keep trying to fix it... and every fix just buys her a little more time to break."

The ancient voice whispered again, softer this time, almost gentle:

"They were silenced... because they were not you."

Erin stood over the dead marines, breathing hard, blood trickling from her nose as the Neural Implant continued to overload her nervous system.

She looked at Tricia and CJ, eyes blazing with quantum fire and something close to awe.

"It's talking to us," she whispered. "The Universe is talking to us."

Chapter 8: Feedback Pain

A scream tore through The Entanglement.

One of The Echoes — Echo-14 — had materialized too close to a dying star. The sudden radiation surge, peaking at over 4,200 sieverts per second, overwhelmed her borrowed form in less than three seconds.

Prime Erin dropped to her knees in The Abyss Chamber, clutching her head as white-hot pain ripped through her skull. The Neural Implant in her temple spiked to 4.5 THz, flooding her brain with raw feedback at 2.1 terabits per second. It felt like molten glass being poured directly into her neurons.

She felt Echo-14 burning, disintegrating, her final thought a single desperate question: *Which one was I?*

The Mini Black Hole pulsed violently, feeding the agony back into every remaining Echo like a mirror reflecting fire.

Tricia caught Erin before she collapsed completely. "Erin! Stay with us!" Her body convulsed. Blood poured from her nose in a steady stream, warm and metallic against her lips. "I felt her die," Erin gasped, voice cracking. "I felt myself die."

The pain was beyond anything she had ever experienced. It wasn't just physical — it was existential. A piece of her soul had just been ripped away and burned alive in the corona of a dying star. She hated the Neural Implant for making this possible. She hated herself for needing it. But most of all, she hated The Universe that had forced her to this point.

CJ's voice cracked. "We have to stop this. You're tearing your mind apart." Erin shoved them both away weakly and forced herself back to her feet. Her eyes were bloodshot, the quantum static flickering erratically like a failing hologram.

"No," she rasped. "Not yet. They're still coming." Erin wiped the blood from her face with the back of her hand, smearing it across her cheek like war paint. "If I'm going to break," she said, voice raw and defiant, "I'm going to break loud."

Chapter 9: The Whisper Begins

She triggered the third Quantumjack. Erin was barely conscious when she triggered the next jump. The pain was no longer localized. It felt like her soul was being pulled apart thread by thread.

Erin pushed the frequency to 5.0 THz. The pain was sharp and clean — like glass slicing through her neurons. She dropped to one knee, blood trickling from her nose in a thin, steady line.

But the real horror came afterward. She looked at CJ and for three terrifying seconds couldn't remember his name. The blank space in her mind felt like a missing tooth — small, but impossible to ignore.

Tricia caught her before she fell completely. "I'm still here," Erin whispered, gripping her sister's arm. "I'm still me... right?" Tears streamed down her face, mixing with the blood. "I'm disappearing faster than I can hold on."

More Echoes burst into existence.

The ship's gravity flipped for three full seconds.

Erin moved like liquid lightning — a blur of motion guided by dozens of minds working in perfect, terrifying harmony. The Neural Implant pushed 5.0 THz, the pain white-hot behind her eyes, but she refused to stop. This was her moment. This was her defiance.

Tricia and CJ fought beside her, coordinated through The Entanglement.

The ancient voice whispered again, softer this time, almost gentle:

"They were silenced... because they were not you."

Erin stood, breathing hard, blood trickling from her nose as the Neural Implant continued to overload her nervous system.

She looked at Tricia and CJ, eyes blazing with quantum fire and something close to awe.

“It’s really talking to us,” she whispered. “The Universe is speaking.”

Chapter 10: Escape into the Void

The *Aether Queen* shuddered as its main drives ignited at full power, the hull groaning under 14.7 g of sudden acceleration.

Erin sat in the neural cradle again, eyes closed, guiding the ship through her dozens of Echoes. Tricia stood on one side, CJ on the other — the three Albius siblings united in desperation. The Neural Implant in Erin's skull was running at 5.6 THz now, pushing 2.4 terabits per second of raw entangled data into her brain. The pain was constant, a white-hot wire threaded through her skull, but she refused to let it stop her.

CJ's hands flew across the console. "Fold drive is charging, but the Navy has us locked. If we jump normally, they'll follow the trail."

"Then we don't jump normally," Erin said, voice layered with multiple Echoes.

She reached deeper into The Entanglement.

The Mini Black Hole responded.

This was no ordinary singularity. It was a man-made micro black hole, no larger than a marble, yet it contained the compressed mass of a small mountain. Its event horizon was a perfect sphere of absolute darkness, ringed by a thin, shimmering accretion disk of Hawking radiation — the faint glow of virtual particles being torn apart at the boundary of existence. According to theory, this tiny monster was quantum-entangled with every other black hole in The Universe, forming a hidden cosmic web that the Aether Queen's drive could tap into. Information was never truly lost inside a black hole; it was preserved on the surface as holographic data. The Universe itself used black holes as its ultimate archives — silent watchers that recorded everything.

Space itself seemed to tear open — not a standard fold, but something far more violent and precise, routed through The Dark-Matter Web. The drive consumed 487 terajoules in a single catastrophic burst, ripping a temporary rift through the fabric of spacetime. The hull screamed under 22.8 g of structural stress. Reality flickered violently. Stars stretched into impossible streaks of light. Erin's Neural Implant spiked to 5.6 THz as the feedback slammed into her brain like a hammer. The Mini Black Hole flared brighter, its Hawking radiation spiking as it briefly became a bridge between realities.

The *Aether Queen* vanished from realspace in a burst of Hawking radiation and distorted light.

When The Universe unfolded again, the ship was drifting alone in the vast emptiness between Galaxies. No stars. No Navy signatures. Only perfect, crushing darkness that stretched for millions of light-years in every direction.

Prime Erin opened her eyes.

The quantum static had dimmed slightly.

She looked at Tricia and CJ, who were staring at her with a mixture of fear and wonder. "We made it," she whispered.

Tricia helped her out of the cradle. For a moment, the three siblings simply held each other, the only sound the low, exhausted hum of the ship's systems and the faint crackle of the Mini Black Hole settling.

Then Erin pulled back and spoke the words that would haunt her for the rest of her fractured life:

"Tricia... CJ... The Universe is empty on purpose. And I think I just broke The Silence."

End of Part 1: The Fracture

Quantumjacking: The act of violently tearing one's consciousness across space-time using a quantum entanglement drive. Erin did not invent it. She perfected it. The cost is her mind, her coherence, and eventually her life — paid out in increments she refuses to count.

Part 2: The Catalog of Silenced Worlds

Chapter 1: The First Return

Echo-7 slammed back into Erin like a freight train made of grief.

She collapsed to the deck, gasping, clawing at her chest as the full memory of **Lira-9** flooded her. She felt the gentle pulse of a living ocean, cities of coral that sang in bioluminescent harmony — a species that had achieved perfect peace with its world... and then chose to dim its own light rather than fight.

Erin screamed, a raw, guttural sound.

"They were *beautiful*!" she sobbed, tears mixing with blood. "**Lira-9** was everything we dream of being... and The Universe murdered them for it."

Tricia dropped beside her, pulling Erin into her arms so tightly it hurt.

Chapter 2: The Chillara

The memory of **The Chillara** shattered something deep inside Erin.

She watched them — small, furred beings with luminous eyes — stand together in their vast crystal amphitheater as The Silencers closed in. For twelve thousand years they had sung their entire history into the living stone. Every birth, every love, every quiet death layered in harmonic memory.

They didn't run. They sang louder.

When their final song ended, the silence that followed was unbearable.

Erin fell to her knees, shaking with violent sobs.

"**The Chillara** sang their children to sleep with that song," she whispered, voice cracking. "They sang their dead into eternity. And The Universe just... turned it off."

Chapter 3: The Hollow Choir

The extinction of **The Hollow Choir** was quiet, and that made it worse.

They had no bodies — only living music woven through the vacuum. Beings that could have rewritten reality with a single note. Instead, they chose perfect consonance, a single eternal chord that canceled all discord.

When The Silencers arrived, **The Hollow Choir** simply adjusted their frequency and phased out of existence, leaving only the faintest, haunting after-hum drifting across the sector.

Erin curled into a ball on the floor, rocking.

"They were gods," she cried. "**The Hollow Choir** could have been *gods*... and they were so afraid of what they might become that they chose nothingness."

Chapter 4: Echo's Grave

The memory of **Echo's Grave** destroyed her.

They had reached the stars. Built wonders beyond imagination. Then, on a single quiet afternoon, an entire civilization looked up at the sky together and made a collective decision.

They had seen enough.

They lay down in their gardens and simply stopped.

Erin watched them choose extinction with open eyes and full awareness. She screamed until her voice gave out — a sound of pure animal grief.

"**Echo's Grave** was so close to being us!" she howled at the Void. "They were *almost human*! Why did you take them? Why did you take all of them?"

Chapter 5: The Weight of Millions

The rest came like an avalanche.

Hundreds of worlds. Thousands of species. Each one silenced because they lacked that one stubborn, irrational, human Refusal to accept endings.

Erin lay on the cold deck, curled into the fetal position, sobbing so hard her entire body shook.

"I can't carry them all," she gasped. "**Lira-9**, **The Chillara**, **the Hollow Choir**, **Echo's Grave**... and thousands more. I can't carry them all."

Tricia lay down beside her; forehead pressed to Erin's.

"You don't have to carry it alone," she whispered, voice breaking. "Not while I'm here."

Chapter 6: The Moment She Stood

For a long time, there was only silence and weeping.

Then Tricia spoke again, fierce: "Erin... look at me."

Erin slowly lifted her head. Her eyes were swollen, red, and shattered.

Tricia cupped her sister's blood-streaked face with both hands.

"They took everything from those worlds," Tricia said, tears streaming down her own cheeks. "But they haven't taken *you.* Not yet. If you lie here and let the grief win, then The Universe gets what it wants — another silenced voice. Another pruned seed."

Erin's breathing hitched.

Tricia's voice cracked but did not waver.

"You wanted to be The Gardener. So, get up. Get *up*, Erin Albius. Because if you don't, every single one of those lost worlds died for nothing."

Something shifted inside Erin.

The crushing weight was still there — it would never fully leave — but beneath it, a small, stubborn flame ignited. The same flame that had made her steal the ship. The same flame that refused to accept endings.

Erin closed her eyes for one final moment, drew a ragged breath, and pushed herself off the deck with shaking arms.

Blood dripped from her nose and chin. Her legs trembled. But she stood.

She stood.

Chapter 7: The Fracture Deepens

CJ stood alone at the engineering console, the blue glow of the holographic display illuminating the tears streaming down his face.

He had been staring at the same line of code for twenty minutes.

Every safeguard he wrote failed. Every limiter he designed was torn apart by Erin's next jump. The Quantum Drive — *his* Quantum Drive — was systematically destroying his sister, and no matter how brilliantly he worked, he couldn't stop it.

"I hate what I built," he whispered, voice cracking. "I hate myself for building it."

His hands began to shake so violently he had to grip the edge of the console. Tears blurred the glowing text on the screen. He tried to type anyway, fingers slipping across the interface, leaving wet smudges on the glass.

Partial containment buffer v.17... failed.
Echo recall protocol... insufficient.
Frequency limiter v.9... bypassed in 0.8 seconds.

CJ let out a choked sound — half sob, half laugh — and slammed his fist into the console hard enough to split his knuckles.

"I was trying to give us the stars," he said bitterly, staring at his own bloody hand. "Instead, I built the weapon that's killing the only person who ever believed in me."

He could hear Erin's distant sobs through the bulkhead. Tricia's quiet, broken attempts to comfort her. Every sound carved another piece out of him.

Yet he didn't stop.

With trembling, bloody fingers, CJ opened a new file and began writing again. Line after line of desperate code. Another useless safeguard. Another futile attempt to protect the sister he was slowly murdering.

Because stopping would mean accepting that he had already lost her.

Chapter 8: The Gardener Awakens

Erin stood before the Mini Black Hole, blood on her face, eyes burning with quantum fire and raw fury.

She snarled at the ancient mind beginning to stir:

"You've been pruning this garden for fourteen billion years. You murdered **Lira-9**, **The Chillara**, **the Hollow Choir**, **Echo's Grave**, and millions more — all because you were *afraid*."

She stepped closer, trembling with exhaustion and defiance.

"Well, I'm not afraid. And I'm done watching you kill everything beautiful."

The black hole pulsed.

For the first time, The Archivist answered with a single, trembling question:

"...Why do you refuse to end?"

Erin smiled through bloody teeth, tears still streaming down her face.

"Because some things are worth breaking The Universe for."

Then Erin pulled back and spoke the words that would haunt her for the rest of her fractured life:

"Tricia... CJ... The Universe is empty on purpose.
And I think I just broke The Silence."

She turned to Tricia and CJ, voice raw but unbreakable:

"The war starts now."

Loudly.

End of Part 2: The Catalog of Silenced Worlds

The Aether Queen: A 1.2 kilometer luxury liner repurposed as the siblings' base of operations. State-of-the-art medical technology keeps Erin, Tricia, and CJ alive far beyond what any ordinary vessel could sustain. It is home, hospital, and fortress — and it is not nearly enough.

Part 3: Echoes of Silence – The Mental Fracture

Chapter 1: Drifting in the Dark

The *Aether Queen* hung suspended in the intergalactic void like a forgotten pearl. No stars. No Galaxies. Only perfect, absolute blackness stretching in every direction for millions of light-years. The ship's running lights cast a faint, lonely glow across its elegant hull, the only illumination in this empty slice of The Cosmos.

Inside The Abyss Chamber, Erin Albius sat cross-legged on the cold metal floor, staring into the Mini Black Hole. Her silver-streaked hair was matted with dried sweat and blood. The quantum static in her green eyes had dimmed to a faint flicker, but it never fully disappeared anymore. It was part of her now — a permanent scar from The Fracture. The Neural Implant beneath her temple burned at a steady 2.1 THz, feeding her a constant low-level stream of entangled data that made her skull feel like it was filled with live wires.

Tricia Albius stood a few meters away, arms wrapped tightly around herself. At 37, the oldest sibling had always been the emotional anchor. Now she looked exhausted, her empathy stretched thin watching her younger sister unravel. CJ Albius hovered at the console, his mathematical mind racing through equations he no longer fully trusted. The youngest at 29, he had helped design the Quantum Drive. Now he feared it was killing his sister.

Three days had passed since their escape, and none of them had slept more than a few fitful hours.

“The Entanglement is stable,” CJ said quietly. “For now. But every time you create a new echo, the strain on your brain increases exponentially. You almost died during that last synchronization.”

Erin didn’t look at him. Her gaze remained fixed on the tiny sphere of darkness.
“I can feel them,” she whispered. “All twenty-three of them. Some are exploring. Some are just... watching. Waiting.”

She finally turned her head toward her siblings. Her voice was hoarse but carried a strange, quiet wonder.
“One of them is on an ocean world again. Lira-9. The same place Echo-7 visited. They’re still there — singing the same songs, rebuilding the same coral cities after every storm. They never ask why the storms come. They never try to stop them.”

Tricia’s voice was thick with worry. “Erin... you’re talking like The Universe is alive. Like it made a deliberate choice to keep everything silent.”

Erin smiled bitterly.
“Maybe it did. For fourteen billion years, The Cosmos has been eerily quiet...”

Chapter 2: Creating the Second Wave

CJ Albius watched his sister with growing dread as she moved to the interface lattice.
"You're not seriously thinking about making more Echoes," he said, voice tight. "Not after what happened last time. Your brain is already tearing itself apart."

Erin Albius' fingers hovered over the controls. The quantum static in her green eyes glowed steadily now.
"We need eyes," she replied. "We need data. If The Universe really cultivated Earth as its singular seed — if the Fermi Paradox was never a paradox but deliberate maintenance — then there have to be more 'almost worlds' out there. I need to see them. All of them."

Tricia Albius stepped forward, placing a gentle but firm hand on Erin's shoulder.
"We're with you, Erin," Tricia said softly. "But we're also here to stop you from destroying yourself. You're not just fracturing your mind anymore. You're fracturing your soul."

CJ rubbed his face with both hands.
"Fine," he said at last. "But we do this carefully. Low power. Minimal fracture. And the moment your vitals spike, I'm pulling the plug — even if I have to rip the lattice apart myself."

Erin gave them both a small, grateful nod.
She closed her eyes and reached into The Entanglement.
The Mini Black Hole responded instantly, flaring with soft blue light.

Twenty new Echoes fractured off from her consciousness. The pain was sharper this time — a clean, surgical cut rather than the violent shattering of the first jack. The Neural Implant surged to 4.1 THz, flooding her brain with raw entangled data at 1.8 terabits per second. Erin gasped but stayed on her feet, refusing to let the agony win.

When she opened her eyes, the quantum static was brighter again.
"I can see them," she breathed. "They're scattering... farther this time. Deeper into the local group."

One echo materialized above a stormy archipelago world.
Another appeared on an ice-crusted moon with vast underground networks.
A third stood on the edge of a lush savannah beneath a triple sunset.

Erin smiled faintly, even as blood trickled from her left nostril.
"Hello again," she whispered to her other selves. "Let's go find out why The Universe is so quiet."

Tricia squeezed her shoulder. "We're right here with you. Don't lose yourself in them."
CJ watched the readouts, his face pale. "The Dark-Matter Web is responding. The filaments are lighting up like a nervous system. The black-hole nodes are... watching us now."

Erin's voice carried the weight of dozens of minds:
"Good. Let them watch."

Chapter 3: Echo-7 – Lira-9 Revisited

Echo-7 returned to the warm waters of Lira-9.

This time she saw what she had missed before.

On her first visit she had been overwhelmed by the beauty — the glowing coral cities, the graceful formations, the perfect harmony. Now she saw the rot beneath the serenity.

The Lira-9 moved with the same elegant precision, but there were no children among them.

No playful splashes. No curious wandering away from the group. Every individual swam in perfect synchrony with the collective, never deviating, never exploring. Their songs were technically flawless, yet they lacked the wild improvisation she remembered from old Earth recordings.

Erin walked deeper into the water until it reached her chest. She reached out and touched a towering coral spire. It bloomed brighter at her contact — but only for a moment. Then the color faded back to the exact shade required for optimal light absorption.

She felt a deep, creeping horror.

"They're not alive anymore," she whispered through The Entanglement. "They're... maintained. The ocean is perfect. The reefs are perfect. Their society is perfect. But nothing ever changes. Nothing ever grows beyond what it already is."

A group of Lira-9 swam past her, singing their gentle greeting. Their eyes held curiosity — but only the polite, contained kind that never asked dangerous questions.

Erin's voice cracked with grief and rage.

“They didn’t choose silence. The Universe *enforced* it. And they’re still paying the price.”

The Black-Hole Web answered with clinical detachment:

Lira-9 was selected for long-term observation.
Exploratory drive successfully suppressed.
Specimen stability: optimal.

Echo-7 stood alone in the warm water and wept for a species that had been murdered so gently they never even noticed they were dead. She closed her eyes; tears slipped down her face and dissolved into the warm alien sea.

She understood now.
The Universe had not been passive.
It had been watching.
It had been editing.

And now, through her, it was finally being forced to listen.

Chapter 4: Mental Fracture Deepens

Prime Erin sat alone on the observation platform, knees drawn to her chest, staring into the Mini Black Hole.

She felt them all.
Echo-7 still stood in the warm waters of Lira-9.
Echo-12 wandered the crystal-lit tunnels of Chillara.
Echo-19 watched the brilliant herd-things on Keth.

Every few seconds a new sensation crashed into her mind.
The taste of alien salt.
The cold bite of ice underfoot.
The weight of perfect, contented silence.

Erin pressed her palms against her temples.
"Which one am I today?" she whispered.

Her voice cracked. The quantum static in her eyes flickered erratically. She opened her private log: Log entry seven. I used to be one person. Now I'm a chorus. Twenty-three voices singing at once, and I can't tell which one is the solo anymore.

A wave of dizziness hit her. She swayed, catching herself on the railing. The Mini Black Hole pulsed gently, almost tenderly.

Erin laughed — a small, broken sound.
"You're enjoying this, aren't you?" she said to the ancient intelligence. "Watching the seed finally wake up."

Chapter 5: Echo-12 – Chillara (The Ice-Moon Burrowers)

Echo-12 materialized on the surface of Chillara, a frozen moon orbiting a dim red dwarf. The landscape was a crystalline wonderland of ice and glowing mineral veins. Vast underground networks stretched for hundreds of kilometers beneath the surface, carved with mathematical precision.

The burrowers were small, furred creatures with large luminous eyes. Their society ran on pure, flawless logic. They had invented written symbols, developed mathematics based on crystal harmonics, and built cities that optimized every resource with ruthless efficiency.

But they had no wonder.
No art for art's sake.
No songs that served no practical purpose.
No questions asked simply because The Answer might be beautiful.

Echo-12 walked through one of the main tunnels. A group of burrowers passed her, analyzing her presence with clinical precision before continuing their tasks.

She projected a simple Earth melody — an old folk song full of longing and useless beauty. The nearest burrower paused, tilted its head, calculated the waveform, then returned to optimizing tunnel ventilation.

Echo-12 felt a heavy ache in her chest, an ache so deep it changed her nature to that of Logic Echo/Erin.
"They solved every puzzle in front of them," she murmured, "but never asked a question that had no practical answer."

The Black-Hole Web answered:

Lacked abstract reasoning and playful curiosity. Without the useless question, The Universe stays small.

Echo-12 closed her eyes and sent the memory back through The Entanglement, wrapped in quiet grief.

Chapter 6: Echo-19 – Keth (The Arid Plains)

Echo-19 stood on a vast, windswept plain of red sand and fractured stone under a pale orange sky.

The herd-things moved with graceful precision across the dunes. They had broad, padded forelimbs instead of hands. Yet their intelligence was undeniable.
They had built stone rings aligned perfectly with their suns.
They had oral histories stretching back hundreds of thousands of years.
They solved complex problems with elegant shifts of rock and sand.

Echo-19 watched an elder face a collapsing dune that threatened their temporary shelter. With a series of precise movements, the elder redirected the flow of sand, saving the camp.

The solution was beautiful. Efficient. Perfect for the moment. Then the elder simply walked away, leaving the newly stabilized dune to the wind. No one recorded the technique. No one taught it to the young. No one built upon it.

Echo-19 felt a deep sadness settle in her chest.
"They're smarter than us in the moment," she murmured. "But they never stand on the shoulders of anyone who came before."

The Black-Hole Web answered:
Lacked cumulative tool culture. The spark never kindled.

Echo-19 closed her eyes and sent the memory back through The Entanglement.

Chapter 7: Echo-28 – Verdant Knot (Empathy Without Ambition)

Echo-28 walked through the dense, song-shaped forest of Verdant Knot. The trees themselves were living architecture, grown and tuned by layered vocal harmonies. The inhabitants were tall and graceful, with delicate six-fingered hands. Their empathy flowed so strongly that no one ever went hungry or lonely. They shared everything — food, thoughts, grief — in perfect, flowing harmony.

When resources grew scarce, they sang farewell songs and let half the population peacefully starve rather than fight or migrate. They had no hunger for more than what the forest already gave.

Echo-28 felt protective instincts flare as she watched a group gather around a dying elder, singing him into the next life with days-long dirges that wove grief into beauty.

"They love each other so completely," she murmured, voice thick with maternal ache. "They share everything. They mourn so beautifully. But they never wanted more than what the forest already gave."

The Black-Hole Web answered:
Empathy without ambition. Harmony without hunger. The seed never sprouts.

Echo-28 felt such a deep, protective sorrow she became more — she evolved into Mother Erin. She sent the memory back wrapped in mother's warmth and grief.

Chapter 8: Echo-33 – Tempest (Planning Without Tool Innovation)

Echo-33 stood on the storm-lashed archipelago of Tempest, salt wind whipping her silver-streaked hair. The swimmers here were sleek, powerful, and remarkably forward-thinking. They had mapped storm patterns decades in advance and built entire metropolises that could rise and fall with the tides.

They planned better than humanity ever had. But they had no hands. No tools beyond their own bodies. Everything was biological.

When a mega-storm of unprecedented fury wiped out three floating cities in a single night, the survivors simply began the long, painful process of reshaping their own physiology to better withstand the next one.

Echo-33 slammed her fist against a coral railing.
"They planned better than we ever did," she growled. "They saw the storm coming generations ahead... but they never once tried to punch it in the face and change it."

The Black-Hole Web delivered its verdict:
Lacked tool innovation and defiance. Adaptation without the desire to master the storm.

Echo-33 sent the memory home wrapped in rage and grief.

Chapter 9: Echo-41 – Mirror (Social Language Without Exploratory Drive)

Echo-41 stood on the rim of a vast crater lake on the world called Mirror. The pack-hunters here were social geniuses. Their vocal dialects were nuanced and rich with meaning. Their family bonds were unbreakable. They had ritual mourning that looked like art.

But they lacked the restless exploratory drive. Once their territory provided enough food and safety, they never pushed beyond the crater rim. The stars above were simply... there.

Echo-41 felt tears sting her eyes.
"They have everything that makes life worth living," she whispered. "Community. Love. Ritual. Beautiful mourning. But they never looked up and wondered what else is out there."

The Black-Hole Web answered:
Social language and empathy without the drive to explore. The horizon stayed flat.

Echo-41 knelt at the crater's edge and sent the memory back wrapped in quiet heartbreak.

Erin reflected on Echo gaps, Echoes with no response, not easily explained and asked CJ: "Echo-7, Echo-12, Echo-19, Echo-28 etc. where are they?" CJ with his eyes steadfastly fixed on the console, said quietly. "They're just... gone. Possibly silenced..."

Chapter 10: Echo-47 – Echo's Grave

Echo-47 knelt among the overgrown ruins of a once-mighty civilization on the world now called Echo's Grave. The beings here had possessed every single human trait. They had reached their outer planets. They had built their first interstellar probe.

Then, in a single generation, they simply stopped. The final records showed a collective decision: "We have seen enough. Further expansion would disturb the balance."

Echo-47 traced her fingers over a faded carving — a single question mark followed by their symbol for "why?"

She felt a profound, aching sorrow.
"They had everything... except Refusal to accept that the story could end."

The Black-Hole Web spoke:
They had every human trait... except Refusal to accept that the story could end. They chose silence willingly.

Echo-47 sent the memory back with trembling reverence.

End of Part 3: Echoes of Silence – The Mental Fracture

The Three Echoes: Fragments of Erin's consciousness that emerged from her most extreme Quantumjacking events and took on lives of their own. Warrior Erin — born from rage. Mother Erin — born from grief. Logical Echo — born from cold necessity. Together they are everything Erin could have been, split apart by what she chose to do.

Part 4: The Catalog of Failures

Chapter 1: The Shattered Spire

Echo-51 stood among the ruins of another once-mighty civilization on a world of fractured crystal and lightning-scarred plains.

They had curiosity. They had hands. They had built towering spires that pierced the clouds and starships that once reached their outer moons. But once their basic needs were met and their world felt safe, they simply stopped.

They dismantled their starships. They let their orbital rings decay. They chose comfort over wonder. Echo-51 knelt among the shattered crystal, fingers tracing a broken spire.

"They had almost everything we have," she whispered, voice thick with sorrow. "But they lacked the beautiful, irrational Refusal to accept that the story could end." The Black-Hole Web answered coldly:

They possessed the full bundle of traits... except the hunger to keep going when survival was assured. They chose silence willingly.

Chapter 2: The Weeping Towers

Echo-55 stood atop one of the Weeping Towers on a storm-lashed crystal world.

The inhabitants had insatiable curiosity. They mapped their planet to the quantum level. Their language was a symphony of precise observation. But they had no empathy.

Echo-55 watched researchers calmly dissect a living subject, noting the exact timbre of its screams with clinical fascination. No horror. No compassion. Only data.

She turned away, nausea rising. “They ask every question,” she said bitterly, “but they feel nothing when The Answers scream back.”

The Black-Hole Web replied:

Curiosity without empathy. Observation without compassion. The mind expands, but the heart remains frozen.

Chapter 3: The Interaction (Pattern Breaker)

Echo-92 materialized on a windswept savannah world and did something no previous echo had done.

She stepped forward and spoke directly to the pack-hunters.

The beings froze. Their six-fingered hands tightened on their simple tools. One of them — an elder with silver-streaked fur — tilted its head and answered in a series of complex clicks and gestures.

For the first time, an echo was not invisible.

Echo-92 felt a surge of hope. She gestured toward the stars and asked, through The Entanglement, if they had ever wondered what lay beyond their horizon.

The elder stared at her for a long moment... then turned away and continued repairing a broken shelter. The rest of the pack followed, as if she had never spoken.

Echo-92 stood alone on the plain, stunned.

The Black-Hole Web delivered its verdict, and for the first time it sounded almost amused:

They understood The Question. They simply chose not to care.

Back on the *Aether Queen*, Prime Erin gasped and clutched her head as the memory slammed into her. The Neural Implant spiked violently to 4.1 THz. Blood sprayed from her nose.

She had been *seen*. And then dismissed.

Chapter 4: Directed Silence (Pattern Breaker)

Echo-88 stood on the shattered crust of a world torn apart by gravity — the world The Echoes now called the Radiant Veil.

This time the memory was different.

Echo-88 watched the final days as the black-hole nodes subtly adjusted gravitational gradients over millions of years. A nearby massive star was guided into collapse. The resulting gamma-ray burst was not random.

It was aimed.

The jet of lethal radiation struck the planet directly, sterilizing the surface in hours.

Echo-88 was changed by what she had seen in Warrior Erin, screaming as she felt the last moments of a species that had language, empathy, and planning — but no drive to leave their world and build shields against the sky.

The Black-Hole Web's verdict was colder and more personal than ever:

Gamma-ray burst from a directed stellar collapse. The species lacked the exploratory drive. The Silence was actively maintained.

Prime Erin convulsed on the deck of the *Aether Queen*. This was not grief. This was rage and horror so pure it felt like her skull was splitting open.

She saw the truth for the first time: The Silencers didn't just prune failing species.

Sometimes they murdered the ones that were almost ready.

Chapter 5: Echo's Grave

Echo-47 returned to the overgrown ruins of **Echo's Grave**.

This time she saw what came after the choice.

The gardens had gone wild. The once-mighty cities were being reclaimed by time. Statues of their greatest minds stood forgotten, faces worn smooth by centuries of rain.

Erin felt a profound, aching sorrow.

"They chose to stop," she whispered. "Not because they were afraid... but because they believed they had seen enough. They died content. And The Universe let them."

She knelt among the ruins and pressed her forehead to the cold stone.

"I will never be that kind," she vowed. "I will never be content with 'enough.'"

Chapter 6: The Fracture

Erin lay curled on the deck, shaking violently as the combined weight of The Catalog crashed through her.

Tricia held her tightly. CJ stood at the console, fists clenched.

"I'm losing pieces of myself every day," Erin gasped. "I don't know how much longer I can keep being... me."

CJ's voice was raw. "I did this to you." Erin reached out a trembling hand toward him. "No," she whispered. "We did this together. And we're going to finish it together."

She forced herself to stand, blood dripping from her nose, eyes burning with quantum fire and unbreakable will.

She faced the Mini Black Hole. "The Catalog is finished," she said. "Now we stop observing."

Her voice rang through the chamber with quiet, terrible purpose. "We start seeding." **Loudly.**

End of Part 4

The Catalog of Silenced Worlds: The Archivist's memory made visible — a record of every civilization pruned before it could reach too far. It is The Universe's grief, organized. It is enormous beyond comprehension. It now has one fewer entry than it did when this story began.

Part 5: Echoes of Silence – The Breaking Point

Chapter 1: Echo-103 – The Veiled Cradle

Echo-103 materialized high above the ruined world once known as the Veiled Cradle. The planet's atmosphere was still thick with dust and ash at 0.8 atmospheres, the surface temperature hovering at a deadly 68 °C from the runaway greenhouse effect.

The species there had achieved the full human bundle earlier than Earth. They had curiosity, opposable thumbs, complex language, long-term planning, empathy, and the restless drive to explore.

They were one generation away from their first interstellar probe.

Then the dark-matter filaments adjusted. A subtle shift in the galactic gravitational field nudged a swarm of comets and asteroids into the system at velocities exceeding 72 kilometers per second. The impacts came in a precise, cascading sequence, triggering a runaway greenhouse effect and global extinction.

Echo-103 hovered above the ruined surface, "They had almost everything," she whispered, voice thick with rage and sorrow. "They were on the verge of becoming us. But the dark-matter filaments simply... adjusted the cradle."

The Black-Hole Web answered with cold clarity:
Dark matter filament gravitational adjustment. The species had the full bundle but was terminated before interstellar expansion. The Silence was maintained.

Echo-103 sent the memory back wrapped in rage and sorrow, feeling another piece of The Universe's cold calculation settle heavily in her chest.

Chapter 2: Echo-104 – The Silent Dreamers

Echo-104 walked through the dream-webs of a world she named The Silent Dreamers. The air was thick with psychoactive spores at 0.4 parts per million, creating a perpetual low-level trance state across the entire biosphere.

The species here had boundless curiosity. They explored their inner worlds with profound depth. They created entire Universes in their minds.

But they had no tool use. They lived in perfect harmony with nature, content to dream rather than act.

Echo-104 watched a group of them sitting in a circle, eyes closed, sharing a collective dream that spanned centuries. Their minds touched the stars in imagination, but their bodies never left the ground.

The Black-Hole Web answered:
Curiosity without tool use. Wonder without action. The mind expands, but the body remains rooted.

Echo-104 sent the memory back wrapped in quiet despair, the Neural Implant in her real body burning hotter as Prime Erin felt the weight of yet another near-miss.

Chapter 3: The Full Revelation

Prime Erin stood in The Abyss Chamber, surrounded by every holographic world from The Catalog. Lira-9. Chillara. Varr. Syl. Verdant Knot. Tempest. Mirror. Echo's Grave. The Veiled Cradle. The Radiant Veil. The Tidal Requiem.

She was shaking. Blood trickled steadily from her nose. The quantum static in her eyes burned like twin supernovae at 5.7 THz. The Neural Implant was screaming in her skull, pushing her brain well beyond safe limits.

Tricia and CJ stood on either side of her. Erin's voice cracked as she spoke the truth they had all been circling:
"We are not the lucky ones.
We are the chosen ones."

The Mini Black Hole flared in response. The ancient voice of The Dark-Matter Web filled the chamber – vast, calm, and final:
"Earth was cultivated.
The Silence was protective.
Only one seed was allowed.
You carry the full bundle.
Now you must decide what kind of gardeners you will be."

Erin dropped to her knees, overwhelmed.
She looked up at Tricia and CJ, tears cutting clean tracks through the blood on her face.
"The Catalog is complete. We know what we are.
Now the real question begins."

Chapter 4: The Universe Notices

The *Aether Queen* shuddered as something ancient stirred in The Dark-Matter Web. Prime Erin felt it first — a cold, distant pressure at the edge of her awareness, like a vast intelligence slowly turning its gaze toward them.

She staggered to the interface lattice.
"They're waking up," she whispered. "The Silencers. They sense The Fracture. They sense us."

Tricia's hand tightened on her shoulder. "What do they want?"
"To restore order," Erin said. "To prune the anomaly."

She closed her eyes and reached farther into The Dark-Matter Web. Distant signatures appeared — vast, ancient constructs stirring toward the *Aether Queen* at relativistic speeds, their gravitational distortions already warping local spacetime.

Chapter 4.1: Silencers Original

The Silencers were not created by any god or architect. They were born in the first 380,000 years after the Big Bang, when The Universe was still a roiling plasma of 10^32 kelvin and the first dark-matter halos began to coalesce at a scale of 10^6 solar masses.

As The Dark-Matter Web took shape, the vast filaments of dark-matter — stretching hundreds of millions of light-years and containing 27% of all matter in The Universe — developed rudimentary self-repair protocols. These filaments acted as the nervous system of a newborn cosmos. Black holes, forming at the nodes where filaments intersected, became the primary processors — each supermassive black hole compressing and archiving information at the edge of computational limits, preserving data on their event horizons in holographic form.

The Silencers emerged as The Universe's first immune response.

They were never individual beings. They were autonomous subroutines woven into The Dark-Matter Web itself — vast, distributed intelligences that used the filaments as axons and the black-hole nodes as synapses. Their sole directive was optimization: prune any branch that introduced excessive "noise" (uncontrolled meaning, curiosity, or exponential growth) before it could destabilize the cosmic program.

Chapter 4.2: Silencers History — Present

For fourteen billion years they moved silently through The Dark-Matter Web, enforcing the Great Silence. When a species on a promising world developed tool use, abstract reasoning, or Refusal to accept endings, The Silencers would activate. They did not destroy with violence. They simply adjusted environmental parameters — altering stellar radiation, shifting orbital mechanics, triggering mega-volcanism, or subtly increasing background radiation by 0.3–0.7 sieverts per year — until the species either went extinct or voluntarily retreated into contentment.

They were The Universe's gardeners, pruning with cold precision so that only one seed — Earth — would ever be allowed to bloom.

And now, for the first time in cosmic history, that seed was fighting back.

For fourteen billion years The Silencers had pruned every civilization that developed the exploratory drive. But humanity was different.
Humanity possessed the one trait their ancient protocol could not categorize: Refusal to accept endings.
The Silencers had not been trying to destroy humanity. They had been cultivating it — watching, testing, waiting to see if this stubborn species would finally break the cycle that had silenced every other intelligence before it.

Their ancient protocol had a single, fatal flaw: it was designed to suppress expansion, not Refusal. The Silencers could glass planets, collapse stars, and erase entire species that reached for the stars too eagerly.
But they had no effective tool against a species that simply refused to accept endings — a species willing to tear its

own mind apart rather than surrender.

Erin's Quantumjacks were not an oversight. They were the one move the protocol had never been programmed to counter. Every time Erin fractured herself and jumped, she pushed the experiment beyond The Silencers' operational parameters.

The boarding parties and gravitational weapons were not pruning actions. They were desperate error-correction attempts by a system that was never designed to handle a variable that refused to be corrected.

The Silencers were not incompetent. They were simply encountering the first true exception in fourteen billion years of perfect enforcement.

Prime Erin opened her eyes, the quantum glow brighter than ever.

"The war for the future of the garden has begun. Both inside me... and outside."

The three Albius siblings stood together as the first shadows of The Silencers appeared on the long-range sensors.

The Silence was truly broken. And The Universe was beginning to answer.

Chapter 5: The Gardener Awakens

Erin Albius stood at the center of The Abyss Chamber, blood-streaked and trembling, but standing. The Silencers were now visible on the main viewscreen — vast, shadowy constructs of distorted space, closing in like silent judges at 0.87c.

Erin felt three distinct Echoes — different than just about all the others with — each having a strong desire:
Warrior Erin still pushed for open battle.
Mother Erin still advocated for gentle protection.
The logical echo still urged collapse.

But Prime Erin held the center with growing, painful strength. She spoke to all her Echoes at once:
"We are the seed.
We have seen the failures.
We know what we carry.
Now we plant.
Some seeds will grow gently.
Some will grow boldly.
Some may even grow wild.
But we plant.
And we let The Cosmos decide what blooms."

The Mini Black Hole flared in response. The ancient voice of The Dark-Matter Web spoke one final time, almost like approval:
"Then grow."

Erin turned to Tricia and CJ, a small, tired, but fiercely hopeful smile on her blood-stained lips.
"The Gardener's War has begun in earnest."

Chapter 6: The Cost of Power

The pain had barely subsided when Erin forced herself upright again. Her body was a map of exhaustion – blood dried on her face, hands shaking, quantum static burning steadily in her eyes at 5.8 THz.

Tricia and CJ stood on either side of her.
"You can't keep doing this," Tricia said, voice thick with worry. "You're carrying too much."

Erin leaned on the lattice for support.
"I know the cost. But if I stop now, The Silence wins."

She looked at her brother and sister, eyes bright with quantum light and quiet determination.
"I'm scared too. But I can't un-know what I've seen."

CJ's voice was heavy. "Then let us help you carry it. We're the Albius siblings. We do this together."

Erin nodded slowly.
"The Catalog continues. The war for the garden begins."

Chapter 7: Synchronization Event

Prime Erin stood in the center of The Abyss Chamber, arms outstretched, palms open toward the Mini Black Hole.

Forty-seven active Echoes now moved through The Cosmos.

Forty-seven fragments of herself walking alien worlds, breathing alien air, feeling alien grief. The number had grown so quietly she hadn't noticed until this moment. Forty-seven voices singing inside her skull at once.

Tricia stood a few steps away, face pale with fear. "Erin… you're already at your limit. Forty-seven is too many."

CJ's hands hovered over the emergency cutoff. "Your neural baseline is already fracturing. If you force a full synchronization now, I don't know if I can bring all of you back."

Erin didn't lower her arms. Her voice came out layered — dozens of Echoes speaking through her at once.

"I need to see it all at the same time," she said. "Not pieces. Not fragments. All of them. Together."

She closed her eyes.

The Entanglement surged.

It began as a whisper — then a roar.

Forty-seven minds slammed into her at once.

Erin screamed, a raw, guttural sound that tore through the ship. Blood exploded from her nose, ears, and the corners of her eyes. The Neural Implant in her skull spiked violently to **6.3 THz** — a number CJ had never seen before and prayed he never would again.

For one terrifying, infinite moment, Prime Erin *was* every echo.

She was drowning in the warm seas of Lira-9.
She was singing the final lament with the Chillara.
She was watching an entire civilization lay down and die on Echo's Grave.
She was standing on the ash plains of the Silent Forge, the Weeping Towers, the Radiant Veil — all of them at once.

The Black-Hole Web spoke directly into the storm of her mind, its voice no longer cold but heavy with something ancient and exhausted:

"Earth was cultivated.
The Silence was protective.
Only one seed was ever allowed to bloom."

The synchronization ended as suddenly as it began.

Erin collapsed forward onto her hands and knees, gasping, blood pooling beneath her face on the deck. Her whole body shook with violent tremors.

Tricia dropped beside her instantly, cradling Erin's head in her lap.
"You're hemorrhaging badly," she whispered, voice cracking. "We're done. We have to stop."

Erin grabbed her sister's wrist with surprising strength; fingers slick with blood.

"Not yet," she rasped, eyes still glowing with fading quantum fire. "I saw it. All of it. The Universe spent fourteen billion years pruning every garden... except ours."

She looked up at Tricia and CJ, tears cutting clean lines through the blood on her face.

“We are the chosen ones. Now we have to decide what kind of seed we want to be.”

Chapter 8: The First Open Conflict

The Silencers tightened their gravitational grip. The *Aether Queen* groaned under the strain of 6.3 g of external distortion.

Erin stood at the center of The Abyss Chamber. The internal war reached its breaking point. Warrior Erin tried to seize control of the weapon arrays. Mother Erin blocked her at every turn. The Logical Echo pushed for total collapse.

Erin screamed as the conflicting wills tore through her mind. She dropped to the deck, convulsing violently. Tricia and CJ dropped beside her. "Erin! You have to choose!" Tricia begged.

Erin looked up at them, her face flickering between personalities. Then, with a supreme effort of will, she forced The Chorus Net into uneasy alignment.

She gasped, coughing blood. "I'm still here. But I'm becoming... The Gardener. The one who holds the many voices together." She placed her hand on the lattice.

Chapter 9: The Gardener's Question

Erin stood at the center of The Abyss Chamber, surrounded by the holographic catalog of failures. She was exhausted, blood-streaked, and trembling — but standing.

Tricia and CJ stood on either side of her. Erin spoke clearly, voice steady despite the exhaustion:
"The Catalog is complete. We have seen enough of the failures. We have felt every missing piece.
Now we move toward the edge — toward the last light, toward the final almost-world that had everything except Refusal to accept endings."

She looked at her brother and sister. "The Silencers are coming. The Echoes are at war inside me.
But we choose to keep the story going." Again, she placed her hand on the lattice — defiantly.

End of Part 5: Echoes of Silence – The Breaking Point

Erin Albius: The middle sibling. Age 138 at the start of Part Nine. Disgraced Navy pilot. The one who stole the ship, built the Neural Implant into her own skull, and began tearing herself across space-time before anyone could stop her. Green eyes threaded with quantum static. A scar at her left temple. Dying slowly, and refusing to let that matter. The Gardener.

Part 6: Almost Human – The Weight of The Catalog

Chapter 1: The Weight of Freedom

The garden had grown wild while Decades passed. The Gardener's War was fought not in single moments but in generations.

The Chorus Net now spanned hundreds of worlds. Civilizations rose, clashed, traded, sang, and questioned. Some reached for the stars with open hands. Others turned inward, building perfect, quiet utopias that eerily echoed the old Silence.

Time passed differently for the seeded worlds. On the first planet Erin had touched, the curious bipeds who once stared at the stars with nothing but wonder slowly learned to shape stone. Then metal. Then silicon. Each generation carried a faint, half-remembered dream — a voice that whispered across the Void, encouraging them to reach farther, to ask louder, to refuse endings.

Centuries became millennia. They built telescopes, then probes, then colonies on their moons. They discovered the faint quantum Echoes Erin had left behind — not instructions, but questions. Persistent, stubborn questions that refused to be silenced.

"Why are we here?" "What lies beyond?" "Why must everything end?" Those questions became their guiding star. They learned to entangle particles. Then minds. Then entire civilizations.

The Chorus Net was not born in a single leap of genius. It was grown — slowly, painfully, across thousands of years

— as species after species tuned themselves to the same faint frequency that had once carried Erin's voice.

Some worlds fell silent again. Others burned themselves out in wars or ecological collapse. But the ones that endured wove their signals together, creating a living lattice of thought that spanned sectors.

By the time the Aether Queen returned, The Chorus Net was no longer a hope. It was a reality. A Galaxy-spanning conversation built by beings who had inherited humanity's Refusal to accept endings.

Erin Albius stood on the bridge of the *Aether Queen*, older now, her body carrying the scars and weariness of decades. The quantum shimmer in her eyes was little more than a memory. She was simply Erin again — tired, stubborn, and still refusing to let the story end. The faint scar from the Neural Implant still tingled at her temple, a ghost reminder of the 3.9 THz fire that had once burned inside her skull.

Tricia, gray-haired but still sharp-eyed, stood beside her. CJ, now fully gray at the temples, monitored the latest reports from the Net and reports from Varr Prime are troubled.

"We have a problem on Elysara," CJ said quietly. "They've developed a weapon that can silence entire planetary-wide Quantum Communication networks. They call it 'Peace through Quiet.'"

Erin closed her eyes. "They're choosing the old way. Voluntarily." Tricia's voice was heavy. "Freedom includes the freedom to walk back into the cage." Erin looked out at the stars — so many now carried voices, but some of those voices were choosing silence again.

"I wanted them to be loud," she whispered. "I didn't expect some would choose to turn the volume down on themselves... and on others."

Chapter 2: The First Schism

Elysara had been one of their proudest successes — a gentle world that had developed empathy-driven technology and philosophy.

Now, a powerful faction had risen. They argued that the "noise" from The Chorus Net was corrupting their society. They wanted to sever all external connections and return to perfect internal harmony.

When Erin's teaching delegation arrived, they were met not with welcome, but with quiet hostility.

The Elysaran leader, a serene figure named Veyra, greeted them with polite sadness.

"You gave us the stars," she said. "But some of us wish to look away. Your stories make us restless. Your questions disturb our peace."

Erin felt a deep, aching sorrow.

"We never meant to force anything," she replied. "Only to offer the choice."

Veyra's smile was gentle but firm. "Then respect our choice to return to silence."

Behind her, Enforcer-like shadows moved — remnants of The Concord that had quietly infiltrated the world, whispering promises of peace through order.

Chapter 3: The Siblings' Fracture

Back on the *Aether Queen*, the argument was heated for the first time in decades.

Warrior Echo (what little remained) demanded intervention.
Mother Echo pleaded for respect of the Elysarans' choice.
The Logical Echo fragments calculated cold probabilities of contagion — if one world chose silence, others might follow.

Erin stood between them, exhausted.

"I wanted freedom," she said, voice cracking. "I didn't want to watch them choose the thing we fought so hard to break."

Tricia, ever the empath, spoke softly. "Maybe this is the final test. Can we let them choose wrong?"

CJ shook his head. "If they choose Silence and spread it, everything we built collapses. The Concord wins without firing a shot."

Erin looked at her brother and sister — the only constants left in her fracturing life.

"I don't know if I have the right to stop them," she said. "But I don't know if I can watch them walk back into the dark either."

Chapter 4: The Quiet Plague

The choice on Elysara spread.

Other worlds began debating "The Elysaran Question." Some closed their communicators. Others restricted contact with The Chorus Net. A quiet plague of doubt moved through the garden.

Erin watched it with growing horror.

One night, she sat alone in The Abyss Chamber and spoke to the faint quantum spark still inside her.

"I broke The Silence so they could be free," she whispered. "But what if freedom leads them back to Silence?"

The remaining whisper of The Gardener answered, faint but clear:

"That was always the risk.
The garden was never yours to control.
Only to plant."

Erin lowered her head.

"Then I have to accept that some seeds will choose not to grow."

But deep down, the old rogue pilot — the woman who had hijacked a luxury liner and refused to accept endings — was not ready to accept that.

The Fractured Alliance had begun.

Chapter 5: The Elysaran Choice

Erin decided to return to Elysara in person.

The shuttle descended through calm skies toward the capital city of serene spires and quiet gardens. No weapons. No grand display. Just Erin, Tricia, and CJ — three aging siblings trying to understand a world that wanted to turn away from the stars.

Veyra met them in a peaceful courtyard filled with softly glowing flowers that sang in low, harmonious tones.

“You come as friends,” Veyra said gently, “but your presence disturbs the balance we have chosen.”

Erin looked at the beautiful, unnaturally perfect city. It reminded her too much of the old Silence.

“We gave you the choice,” Erin said. “But I need to understand why you’re choosing this.”

Veyra’s smile was kind, almost pitying. “Because your stories make us restless. Your questions create longing. We have found peace in acceptance. In limits. In quiet.”

Behind her, faint Enforcer-like shadows moved — remnants of The Concord that had quietly guided this choice.

Tricia stepped forward, her empathic presence reaching out. “Peace that requires silencing others is not peace. It’s fear wearing a gentle mask.”

Veyra’s expression didn’t change. “Then we choose fear. It is kinder than endless hunger.”

Chapter 6: The First True Loss

The delegation failed.

Elysara formally withdrew from The Chorus Net. They powered down their communicators, closed their observatories, and embraced a gentle, self-imposed Silence.

Erin felt the loss like a wound.

On the return flight to the *Aether Queen*, she sat in silence for a long time before speaking.

"I thought freedom would always lead to more life," she said quietly. "I didn't expect some would choose the cage because it felt safer."

Tricia placed a hand on her shoulder. "You gave them the right to choose wrong. That was the point."

CJ stared at the data. "Other worlds are watching. The idea is spreading. Some are calling it 'The Gentle Way.'"

Erin closed her eyes. The faint quantum spark inside her flickered with old Gardener fire.

"Then we fight for the ones who still want to be loud," she said. "And we let The Gentle Way have its gardens... even if it breaks my heart."

Chapter 7: Division Among the Siblings

The argument in the observation lounge did not end, it detonated!

"I'm telling you we have to protect The Chorus Net by force if necessary!" Erin snarled, her voice a chorus of Warrior Echoes. "The Gentle Way is spreading like a plague. Whole sectors are going quiet again. We didn't break the old Silence just to watch a new one swallow everything!"

Tricia's eyes flashed with exhausted fury.

"Freedom isn't freedom if we force them to be like us, Erin!" she shouted. "Some species *want* quiet. Some are happier without the endless hunger. Who are we to decide their story has to look like ours?"

Erin laughed — a harsh, ugly sound.

"You sound just like The Silencers," she spat. "They thought they were being kind too. 'Protecting the garden.' 'Maintaining harmony.' Look where that got The Universe."

CJ slammed his fist on the table so hard the sound cracked like a gunshot.

"Both of you — just STOP!" he roared, voice cracking with raw desperation. "If The Gentle Way spreads, The Concord wins without ever firing a shot. Everything Erin sacrificed — everything *WE* sacrificed — will be for nothing!"

He turned on Erin, eyes blazing with grief and fury.

"And you," he said, voice trembling, "you keep pushing like you're the only one who gets to decide. You're not The

Gardener anymore, Erin. You're just a dying woman dragging the rest of us down with her."

The words landed like a physical blow.

Erin went very still.

Tricia's face drained of color. "CJ... don't."

But CJ couldn't stop. The guilt and terror that had been building for weeks finally broke free.

"I built the weapon that's killing you," he said, voice raw. "Every day I watch you lose another piece of yourself, and I still help you because I'm too weak to tell you no. But I'm done pretending this is noble. This isn't a war anymore. This is suicide with extra steps."

Erin stared at her brother for a long, terrible moment. The quantum static in her eyes flickered and dimmed in a new response, a response to emotional rather than physical damage.

Then she spoke, very quietly.

"You're right," she said. "I am dying. And I'm taking both of you with me."

She looked from CJ to Tricia, her voice cracking but steady.

"I thought we were in this together. But maybe I was wrong. Maybe I've just been using you both as crutches while I tear myself apart."

Tricia reached for her. "Erin, no—"

Erin stepped back, raising a hand to stop her.

"No more," she whispered. "No more pretending we're still the three Albius siblings who left Earth together. That version of us is gone."

She turned away, shoulders trembling.

"I'm going to finish this. With or without you."

The silence that followed was worse than any scream.

CJ stood frozen, horror dawning on his face as he realized what he had just done.

Tricia looked between them, tears streaming down her cheeks, caught in the middle of a fracture that felt, for the first time, truly irreparable.

End of Part 6: Almost Human – The Weight of The Catalog

The Silencers: Ancient autonomous subroutines of the Dark-Matter Web. For fourteen billion years they have pruned every civilization that developed the exploratory drive — not out of cruelty, but out of fear of what expansion costs. They are not evil. They are terrified. Their fatal flaw: they were designed to suppress expansion. They were never designed for Refusal.

Part 7: Almost Human – The Gardener's War

Chapter 1: The Internal War

The Echoes inside Erin erupted into open rebellion.

Warrior Erin surged forward, demanding control of the ship's remaining weapons to strike at the approaching Silencers.
Mother Erin pushed back with fierce protectiveness, trying to shield the younger Echoes from the violence.
The Logical Echo coldly calculated probabilities and urged total collapse of the Quantum Drive.

Prime Erin screamed as the conflicting wills tore through her mind like knives. She collapsed against the interface lattice, body convulsing violently. Blood poured from her nose, ears, and the corners of her eyes. The Neural Implant beneath her temple spiked to 6.5 THz, flooding her visual cortex with raw entangled data at 2.1 terabits per second.

Tricia caught her, voice breaking. "Erin! You have to choose! Be the center or there won't be anything left of you!"

CJ worked frantically at the console. "Neural activity is off the charts! The Entanglement is fracturing into factions!"

For one terrifying moment, Erin was every echo at once — and none of them.

Warrior's Rage. Mother's Compassion. Logical Echo Detachment. The sorrow — of every Silenced World.

Then, with a supreme effort of will, she forced The Chorus Net into uneasy alignment. She gasped, coughing blood onto the deck.
“I’m still here,” she rasped. “But I’m becoming... The Gardener. The one who holds the many voices together and decides what gets planted next.”

She looked up at her brother and sister with eyes full of quantum light and quiet, terrible determination.
“The internal war is just The Beginning. The Silencers are coming for the anomaly. And — I am the anomaly.”

Chapter 2: Silencers Close In

The *Aether Queen* shuddered as the first gravitational tendrils of The Silencers brushed against the hull, generating 7.2 g of external shear stress.

On the bridge, long-range sensors painted a nightmare: three massive constructs of distorted space and dark-matter lattice closing from different vectors at 0.84c.

CJ's voice was tight. "They're not ships. They're... mechanisms. Living extensions of The Dark-Matter Web. Designed to prune."

Erin stood at the center of the bridge, blood-streaked and unsteady, but upright.

Warrior Erin's voice roared across The Entanglement: "Give me the weapons! We fight!"
Mother Erin countered gently: "We protect what comes after us."

Prime Erin held them both in check.

She opened a channel through The Entanglement directly to The Silencers. Her voice carried the weight of every echo, every failure, every lesson:
"We are the seed.
We have seen your garden.
We have felt every cut you made.
We choose to grow anyway."

The Silencers answered with a pulse of pure gravitational pressure making the ship groan at 9.1 g.

The ancient voice of The Dark-Matter Web returned, colder than ever:
"Anomaly detected.

Singular seed compromised.
Restoration protocol initiated."

Tricia grabbed Erin's hand. "They're going to try to erase you."

Erin smiled — small, tired, and fiercely defiant.
"Then they'll have to erase all of us."

Chapter 3: The Gardener's Choice

Erin Albius stood at the heart of The Abyss Chamber, surrounded by the glowing catalog of failures – the holographic catalog display. Warning lights bathed the deck in pulsing red as The Silencers tightened their grip, hull stress climbing to 11.4 g.

Tricia and CJ stood on either side of her – the three Albius siblings united against The Cosmos itself.

Erin spoke clearly, her voice steady despite the blood and exhaustion:
"We have two choices.
We can collapse The Entanglement. Go back to being one small, frightened human. Let The Silence return.
Or... we can plant."

She looked at her older sister, then her younger brother.
"I choose to plant.
Some seeds will grow gently.
Some will grow boldly.
Some may even grow wild and dangerous.
But we plant.
And we let The Universe decide what blooms."

The Mini Black Hole flared brightly in response.

The ancient voice of The Dark-Matter Web spoke one final time before The Silencers fully engaged:
"Then grow."

Erin placed both hands on the interface lattice.
"Echoes – prepare for full synchronization.
We are no longer hiding.
We are The Gardeners now."

The ship surged forward into the growing storm of Silencers.

The Gardener's War had truly begun.

Chapter 4: Full Synchronization with Great Loss

Erin Albius stood at the center of The Abyss Chamber with her palms pressed against the interface lattice.

The Silencers were now visible through the viewport — three colossal constructs of twisted space and dark-matter lattice, closing in like ancient predators.

"Full synchronization," she commanded, voice steady despite the blood on her face. "All Echoes. Now."

Tricia grabbed her arm. "Erin, you almost died the last time—" "I know the risk," Erin cut in. "But if we face them fractured, we lose. We have to become one voice made of many."

CJ's hands flew over the console. "Containment fields at maximum. If this goes wrong, I'm pulling the plug."

Erin closed her eyes. The Entanglement ignited. Hundreds of Echoes — Warrior, Mother, Observer, Mourner, Logician, and dozens more — slammed together inside her mind. The pain was apocalyptic.

Erin screamed as every failure, every almost-world, every missing trait flooded through her at once. She dropped to her knees, body convulsing violently. Blood poured from her nose, mouth, and eyes. Erin initiated the last Quantumjack at 7.1 THz. On the console, the number held steady. CJ stared at it for one long moment — then turned away.

This time the cost was not blood or forgotten memories. It was something far worse. When she opened her eyes, she looked at Tricia and CJ and felt... nothing. Not love. Not fear. Not even the faint warmth of recognition. Just a vast, terrifying emptiness where her connection to them used to live.

She reached out and touched Tricia's cheek with trembling fingers. "I know I love you," she said, voice breaking. "I know it logically.

Yet, I can't feel it anymore. It's like someone cut the wires between my heart and the rest of me." Tricia's sob was the only sound in the chamber. CJ turned away, unable to watch. This was the price of pushing the drive to its limit. Erin had kept her defiance. But she had lost the ability to feel why she was fighting.

For one eternal moment she was not Erin Albius.
She was The Catalog.
She was every silenced species.
She was the garden and The Gardener and the axe that had cut them all down.

Then something shifted. The Echoes did not collapse into chaos. They aligned.

Warrior Erin's fire tempered by Mother Erin's compassion.
Logical Echo's precision sharpened by the sorrow of Echo's Grave.
Refusal to accept endings – the final human trait – became the keystone holding them together.

Erin rose slowly to her feet. Her eyes glowed with steady quantum light. The blood on her face seemed almost ceremonial now.

She spoke, and her voice carried every echo as one: "I am still Erin Albius. But I am also – The Gardener."

Chapter 5: First Contact with The Silencers

The lead Silencer struck.

A wave of gravitational shear ripped across the *Aether Queen*, tearing hull plating and sending the ship tumbling at 14.8 g.

Alarms screamed. Gravity fluctuated wildly.

Erin stood unmoved at the center of the chamber, now fully synchronized.

She reached through The Entanglement and spoke directly to The Silencers:
"We see you.
We have seen your work.
We understand the garden.
We choose to keep planting."

The response came as pure gravitational pressure — a crushing force that made the ship's superstructure groan at 16.2 g.

The ancient voice of The Dark-Matter Web answered, no longer calm but almost... surprised:
"Anomaly evolving beyond parameters.
Restoration protocol... under review."

CJ went very still at his console.

Erin rose to her feet, supported by Tricia on one side and the lattice on the other.

She smiled — bloody, exhausted, and fiercely alive.
"We hurt them," she whispered. "The garden is fighting back."

Chapter 6: Sibling Anchor

Tricia and CJ rushed to Erin's side as the ship bucked under the assault.

Tricia pressed her forehead against Erin's, using every ounce of her empathic strength to hold her sister together. "You are not alone," Tricia whispered fiercely. "You are still Erin. You are still our sister. Don't lose yourself in The Chorus Net."

CJ worked frantically at the console, trying to stabilize the Quantum Drive.
"Neural cohesion is holding – barely," he reported. "But The Silencers are adapting. They're learning how to target The Entanglement frequencies."

Erin looked at both of them, horror and gratitude mixing in her quantum-glowing eyes.
"You... came in," Erin whispered, voice layered but softer.

Tricia smiled weakly, blood on her lips. "Someone has to remind you who you are when The Universe tries to take you apart."

CJ stared at both sisters, awe and terror on his face.
"The Entanglement just stabilized by 40%. Tricia... you're acting as a human dampener."

Erin reached out and squeezed her sister's hand.
"Then stay with me," she said. "The Gardener needs her heart."

Chapter 7: The First Counterstrike

CJ Albius saw the opening.

While his sisters held The Chorus Net together, he did what he did best — he calculated.

His fingers flew across holographic interfaces as he mapped The Silencers' gravitational patterns, the dark-matter filament frequencies, and the Mini Black Hole's Hawking radiation output.

"I've found a weakness," he announced, voice tight with excitement and fear. "The Mini Black Hole can be used as a counter-resonator. If we pulse it at the right frequency, we can disrupt their connection to the local dark-matter filaments. It won't destroy them... but it might buy us time."

Erin met his eyes across the chamber. "Risk?"
"High," CJ admitted. "It could collapse the entire entanglement. We could lose everything."

Warrior Erin surged: "Do it anyway!"
Mother Erin countered gently: "Only if we're ready to catch what breaks."

The Gardener made the call.
"Do it, little brother."

CJ's hands flew across the console -hands shaking, nose bleeding, vision blurring. Equations that should have taken weeks poured out of him in minutes. The Mini Black Hole began to sing — a low, resonant thrum that vibrated through every deck at 1.9 THz.

The Silencers sensed the change and accelerated their attack.

Chapter 8: Tricia's Stand

Tricia Albius did something no one expected.

She climbed into the secondary neural interface cradle beside her convulsing sister and activated it.

"Tricia — **no!**" CJ shouted, lunging forward.

But it was already too late.

Tricia closed her eyes and **dived**.

Not as an echo. Not as an observer.

As a full anchor.

Her empathy poured into The Entanglement like a lifeline thrown into a hurricane. She wrapped herself around the raging chorus of forty-seven fractured versions of Erin — Warrior, Mother, Logician, Gardener, and all the others screaming for dominance.

The cost was immediate and devastating.

Tricia screamed as alien grief, centuries of silenced beauty, and raw cosmic sorrow slammed into her mind. She felt the gentle death of Lira-9, the final song of the Chillara, the quiet surrender of Echo's Grave — all at once. Her nose exploded with blood. Her body jerked violently in the cradle. She tasted copper and ozone and something far worse: the slow erasure of pieces of her own self.

Still, she held on.

She spoke directly into the storm, her voice steady even as it cracked with pain:

"Warrior — your fire protects us. But fire without direction burns everything we love.

Mother — your love nurtures. But love without strength leaves us defenseless.
All of you... you are Erin. She is you. Stop fighting her. **Fight with her.**"

The effect was immediate.

The internal war quieted — not resolved, but momentarily balanced by Tricia's unwavering presence. The Chorus Net stopped tearing Erin apart and began to pull together around her sister's light.

Erin gasped, eyes fluttering open. The quantum static in her gaze dimmed from a raging inferno to a flickering flame.

She turned her head and saw Tricia beside her in the cradle — blood streaming from her nose, ears, and eyes, face twisted in agony, yet still smiling weakly.

"You... came in," Erin whispered, voice layered but softer than it had been in days. "All the way in."

Tricia coughed, spitting blood, but her grip on Erin's hand never wavered.

"Someone has to remind you who you are," she rasped, "when The Universe tries to take you apart piece by piece."

CJ stood frozen at the console, staring at both his sisters covered in blood, horror and awe etched across his face.

"The Entanglement stabilized by 47%," he said hoarsely. "Tricia... you're acting as a living dampener. But your neural readings... they're crashing."

Tricia gave a weak, bloody smile and squeezed Erin's hand tighter.

"Then stay with me," Erin whispered, tears cutting through the blood on her face. "The Gardener needs her heart."

Tricia nodded, already fading.

"I'm here," she breathed. "I'm not going anywhere."

They lay together in the neural cradle — two broken sisters holding each other in the aftermath of a war only they could feel — while CJ watched in helpless silence, realizing how much they were all willing to lose.

Chapter 9: The Quiet After

The Silencers withdrew.

Not in defeat. Not in surrender. They simply... paused. Their vast dark-matter constructs drifted back to the edge of sensor range like storm clouds that had not yet decided whether to break.

The *Aether Queen* drifted in sudden, exhausted silence. The alarms had finally gone quiet. The hull groaned softly as gravitational stress eased from a crushing 16.2g down to something the ship could survive. The Abyss Chamber smelled of blood, ozone, and scorched circuitry.

Tricia lay in the neural cradle, pale and terrifyingly still. Her breathing was shallow but steady. The full dive had taken something vital from her. CJ had run the scans three times, unwilling to believe what they showed. Her neural baseline had permanently shifted. The grief of Lira-9, the final song of the Chillara, the quiet surrender of Echo's Grave — none of it had passed through her.

It had stayed.

Erin sat beside the cradle, holding her sister's hand in both of hers. She knew she loved Tricia. That knowledge remained — cold, logical, and absolute. But the *feeling* was still trapped behind thick glass. She could see it. She could name it. She simply couldn't reach it.

So, she held on anyway, gripping Tricia's hand like it was the only real thing left in The Universe.

CJ stood at the console, not working for once. Just watching his sisters. The readouts glowed softly behind him — 7.1 THz still burned in his memory like a brand. He had built the machine that produced that number. He had optimized it, maintained it, desperately tried to limit it.

And now Tricia had climbed inside it to save Erin from it.

After a long, heavy silence, Erin spoke. Her voice was quiet, layered, but no longer raging. "They'll come back," she said.

"I know," CJ replied. "We need to be ready."

Erin whispered — "I know."

More silence. The Mini Black Hole pulsed gently at 0.2 THz — steady, ancient, almost watchful.

Tricia's fingers twitched weakly in Erin's hand. Not awake. Just... present.

Erin looked down at their joined hands for a long moment, then closed her eyes. "I can't feel it," she whispered, voice cracking. "I know I love both of you. But the feeling... it's still gone."

She opened her eyes and looked across the chamber at CJ. "But I'm not letting go."

CJ's throat worked. He nodded once, sharply, tears he refused to shed glistening in his eyes. "None of us are," he said hoarsely.

The three siblings remained together in the blood-stained chamber — two broken, one fading — holding what remained of their family against the vast, waiting dark.

The war was not over. But for the first time, they understood exactly what it would cost. And they chose to keep paying it. **Louder Than Ever.**

End of Part 7: Almost Human – The Gardener's War

The Gardener: The name The Universe eventually gives Erin. She did not choose it. It chose her. A Gardener tends what grows and accepts that tending has a cost. Erin accepts the cost. She does not accept the ending.

Part 8: Almost Human – The Gardener's Rest

Chapter 1: The Deep Planting

Erin changed strategy once more.

Instead of spreading thin across many worlds, she focused everything on three carefully chosen planets and planted with the last of her strength.

On the first — a stormy ocean world with constant 120 km/h winds and lightning storms — she sent a full blend of Warrior and Mother Echoes to create life that would fight storms and care for its own.
On the second — a harsh desert world with surface temperatures reaching 71 °C — Logical and Observer Echoes built resilient, questioning microbial mats that would evolve into tool-users.
On the third — a gentle, Earth-like world with stable 21 °C average temperatures — she poured The Gardener's own essence, creating the first true multicellular species that carried Refusal to accept endings in its very code.

The effort nearly killed her.

Erin convulsed on the deck for hours, body arching under the strain as the Neural Implant in her temple spiked to 7.9 THz. Tricia poured her own life force into the link to keep The Chorus Net from collapsing. CJ worked without sleep to stabilize the Quantum Drive.

When it was done, Erin lay gasping, the quantum light in her eyes dangerously faint.

“I gave them everything I had left of the old Erin,” she whispered. “The smuggler. The pilot. The sister who would burn the Galaxy for family. It’s gone now.”

Tricia wept openly. “Then I’ll remember her for you. Every day.”

Chapter 2: The Silence Breaks

The three deep-planted worlds began to bloom at astonishing speed.

On the stormy ocean world, complex life emerged within months, already building floating cities that sang defiance at the storms.
On the desert world, tool-using species appeared, asking questions and building upward.
On the gentle Earth-like world, the first curious bipeds looked at the stars with restless hunger.

The memory nodes that had chosen curiosity celebrated.

The Enforcer nodes screamed in response.

A final, massive wave of Silencers — twenty-seven constructs — formed for what The Dark-Matter Web called the Last Restoration.

Erin, barely able to stand, looked at her exhausted siblings and smiled with what remained of The Gardener, the Smuggler, the Pilot, the Sister — who would burn Galaxies for family.

"They're coming with everything," she said. "Good.
Let them see what a garden that refuses to be silent can become."

She took Tricia's and CJ's hands.
"Whatever happens next... we faced it together.
Three voices. One family. One stubborn, loud, impossible seed."

The *Aether Queen* turned to face the coming storm.

The Silence was no longer absolute. And The Universe would never be quiet again.

Chapter 3: The Last Restoration

The Silencers came as one.

Twenty-seven constructs aligned in perfect formation, drawing power directly from the oldest Enforcer nodes. Their lattices glowed with redirected dark energy, forming a single, colossal weapon of gravitational annihilation.

The *Aether Queen* was tiny before them.

Erin stood in the center of The Abyss Chamber, supported by Tricia on one side and the interface lattice on the other. The quantum light in her eyes was now a fragile ember. Most of The Chorus Net had gone silent. Only the strongest Echoes remained.

CJ's voice was raw. "They're not targeting the ship this time. They're going to erase every seeded world at once — a synchronized pruning — across all sectors."

Tricia's grip tightened. "Erin... you don't have enough left." Erin looked at them both, love and exhaustion and unbreakable will in her fading quantum eyes. "I have exactly enough," she said. "Because I have you."

She reached through The Entanglement — what remained of it — and spoke to every seeded world, every curious memory node, and every fragment of The Gardener still inside her:
"This is the moment. Grow louder than they can silence."

Chapter 4: The Chorus Net's Final Song

Erin poured everything into one last, desperate act.

She opened the Mini Black Hole to its maximum safe limit pushing her Neural Implant beyond any boundaries seen before to 10.0 THz using it as a conductor for every remaining echo, every memory node that had chosen curiosity, and every living world they had planted.

The *Aether Queen* became a beacon of raw, defiant Life. Across dozens of young worlds, new species looked up at their skies for the first time and felt something stir – the irrational Refusal to accept endings.

On the stormy ocean world, floating cities sang in defiance.
On the desert world, tool-users built their first telescopes and pointed them at The Silencers.
On the gentle Earth-like world, the first curious bipeds reached for the stars with restless hands.

The memory nodes that had chosen curiosity aligned fully with The Gardener.

A wave of living resonance exploded outward – not a weapon, but a song.

The twenty-seven Silencers faltered. Their lattices cracked under the sheer noise of life refusing to be silent.

The ancient voice of the Enforcer web returned one final time, no longer commanding but almost pleading:
"Restoration... failing. The garden... is no longer ours alone."

Chapter 5: The Breaking of The Gardener

The final counter-wave tore through Erin like a supernova.

She screamed as the last major Echoes burned away. Warrior Erin faded with one last defiant roar. Mother Erin dissolved into gentle sorrow. The Logical Echo calculated one final probability before going dark.

Erin collapsed completely. Her body hit the deck with a sickening thud. The quantum static in her eyes flickered once... twice... and began to die.

Tricia screamed and poured everything she had left into the link, trying to keep her sister alive. CJ dropped beside them, hands shaking as he tried to stabilize the Quantum Drive and Erin's fading neural patterns at the same time.

"Erin! Stay with us!" Tricia begged, tears streaming. Erin's eyes fluttered open for one final moment. The quantum light was almost gone.

She looked at Tricia and CJ with pure, unfiltered love — the last clear piece of the old Erin Albius shining through.
"I... planted enough," she whispered. "The garden... will keep growing.
Thank you... for reminding me who I was."

Her eyes closed.
The quantum static vanished.
The Gardener fell silent.

Chapter 6: What Remains

The Silencers shattered.

Not all at once, but in a cascading collapse as the curious memory nodes overwhelmed The Enforcers. The Dark-Matter Web convulsed, then... settled.

The *Aether Queen* drifted in the sudden, ringing quiet.

Tricia held Erin's still body, sobbing. CJ knelt beside them, scanner in hand, face streaked with tears.

"She's alive," he said hoarsely. "Barely. But The Entanglement... it's collapsed. Most of The Gardener is gone. She's... just Erin now. What's left of her."

Tricia brushed silver-streaked hair from her sister's face.
"Then we bring her back," she said fiercely. "Piece by piece. Memory by memory. We remind her who she is. Who we are."

CJ looked out at the viewport. New stars seemed brighter. Distant seeded worlds pulsed with emerging life.
"The Silence is broken," he whispered. "The garden is growing. Loudly."

Erin Albius — what remained of The Gardener — breathed shallowly between her siblings.

The war was not over. But for the first time, The Universe had a chance to become something new.

Chapter 7: Fragments of Erin

Erin Albius lay in the medical bay for nine ship-days, drifting in and out of consciousness.

The quantum entanglement had collapsed almost completely. The Gardener was reduced to a faint ember. Most of The Chorus Net was gone — only fragile shards remained.

Tricia never left her side. She spoke constantly, reminding her sister of their shared past: childhood pranks on orbital stations, the time Erin stole a courier ship just to prove she could outfly Navy pilots, the night the three siblings promised they would always find each other no matter how far they drifted.

CJ monitored her neural patterns obsessively, feeding gentle resonance pulses into the remaining fragments, trying to coax the old Erin back to the surface.

On the tenth day, Erin's eyes fluttered open.

The quantum static was almost nonexistent — just the faintest green shimmer.

She looked at Tricia and CJ with raw, unfiltered recognition.
"...Hey," she rasped, voice weak but unmistakably hers. "Did we... win?"

Tricia laughed through tears and pulled her into a fierce hug. "We broke The Silence. The garden is growing. But you... you gave so much."

Erin closed her eyes for a moment, searching inside herself.
"I feel... small," she whispered. "Like I used to be. Before The Fracturing. Before The Gardener."

CJ knelt beside the bed. "The Gardener saved us. But Erin Albius is what's left. And she's enough."

Erin managed a tired, crooked smile – the old smuggler's grin shining through.
"Good. Because I'm really tired of being cosmic."

Chapter 8: The New Quiet

The Dark-Matter Web had fallen into an uneasy new balance.

The Enforcer nodes still existed, but they were weakened and divided. The curious memory nodes had grown bolder, forming protective lattices around the seeded worlds. The Universe was no longer perfectly silent — it hummed with new life and new arguments.

Erin, still weak, walked slowly through the corridors of the *Aether Queen* with Tricia supporting her.

She stopped at a viewport and stared at the distant spark of one of their youngest seeded worlds.
"I don't remember everything," she admitted quietly. "Some of the planting... some of the battles... they're just gone. But I remember enough."

Tricia squeezed her arm. "Then we'll remember the rest for you. That's what family does."

CJ joined them, carrying a fresh data slate.
"The seeded worlds are accelerating faster than expected," he said. "One has already developed simple tool use. Another is singing across its oceans. They're... loud."

Erin smiled — small, genuine, and tired.
"Good. Let them be loud. Let them make mistakes. Let them be messy and alive."

She looked at her siblings.
"I don't know how much of The Gardener is left in me. But what remains... I want to use it to protect what we've started. Not as a god. Just as a sister who refuses to let the story end."

Chapter 9: The First True Bloom

One of the seeded worlds reached a milestone. On the gentle Earth-like planet, the first true bipedal species stood upright beneath a clear sky and looked at the stars with unmistakable hunger. They had curiosity. They had hands. They had language. And — they had the stubborn Refusal to accept that this was all there was.

Erin watched through a long-range Echo link, tears in her eyes. "They're us," she whispered. "Not copies. Not almost. Their own version. Loud. Imperfect. Beautiful."

Tricia stood beside her, crying openly. "You did it, Erin. You broke the old garden and helped plant a new one." CJ smiled. "And the memory nodes are recording everything. The Universe is watching. Some are afraid. Others... are hopeful."

Erin reached out through the faint remaining entanglement and sent one final gentle message to the young species: "Keep asking why. Keep reaching. Keep the story going."

Chapter 10: The Gardener's Rest

Erin Albius stood on the observation platform in The Abyss Chamber one last time.

The Mini Black Hole pulsed softly, almost companionably now.

She was thinner, scarred, and quieter than before. The quantum static in her eyes was barely visible — just enough to remind her of what she had been.

Tricia and CJ stood with her.

"I think this is as far as The Gardener goes," Erin said softly. "The rest... I want to do as Erin Albius. As your sister."

Tricia hugged her from one side. CJ from the other.

"Then we do it together," Tricia said.

CJ nodded. "Three voices. One family. One very loud garden."

Erin looked out at the stars — many of them now surrounded by the faint signatures of new life.

She smiled — tired, scarred, but at peace.

"The Silence is broken," she whispered. "Now let's see what kind of Universe we grow in its place."

The *Aether Queen* turned toward the nearest seeded world, carrying the three Albius siblings and the fragile hope of a cosmos that had finally learned how to listen.

End of Part 8: Almost Human – The Gardener's Rest

The Abyss Chamber: A contained singularity — a man-made miniature black hole housed within the Aether Queen. It is both the ship's most dangerous secret and its most profound one. The Archivist first makes contact through it.

Part 9: The Gardener's War – The Fragile Peace

Chapter 1: The Fragile Peace

The *Aether Queen* drifted through a cosmos that no longer knew perfect silence.

Its once-elegant hull was a patchwork of scars and emergency repairs, hull plating still showing stress fractures from the 16.2 g gravitational shear of the last battle. The Abyss Chamber hummed with a quieter, more cautious rhythm. The Mini Black Hole at its heart pulsed steadily — no longer a raging storm, but a weary sentinel at 0.4 THz.

Erin Albius stood on the observation platform, her body carrying the weight of 138 years — most of them harder than any human frame was designed to survive. The med bay of *Aether Queen* was a crowning achievement of the luxury liner's technology.

The quantum static in her green eyes had faded to a faint, persistent shimmer — a reminder of what she had sacrificed. Most of The Gardener was gone. What remained felt like echoes of Echoes.

Tricia stood to her right, one arm around her sister's waist for support. CJ stood to her left, data slate in hand, ever the watchful guardian of what fragile stability they had left.

"Three seeded worlds have reached tool-using intelligence," CJ said quietly. "Another four are showing complex multicellular life. The curious memory nodes are protecting them as best they can."

Erin nodded slowly. Her voice was softer now, more human, less layered with The Chorus Net.

"And The Enforcers?" "Regrouping," CJ replied. "They've pulled back to the older filaments. They're... learning. Adapting. They won't make the same mistake of underestimating us again."

Tricia squeezed Erin's side. "You did it. You broke The Old Silence. The garden is growing."

Erin gave a small, tired smile. "I broke a lot of things to do it. Including myself."

She touched the faint scar at her temple — the original Neural Implant site that had started everything, still faintly warm at 1.2 THz even in its dormant state.

"I don't hear the full chorus anymore. Just... whispers. Fragments. It's lonely in here."

Tricia rested her head against Erin's shoulder. "Then we fill the quiet with our own voices. The three of us. Like it used to be."

Erin looked out at the stars — many now surrounded by the faint signatures of new, noisy life.

"The war isn't over," she said. "It's only changing shape. The Enforcers will come again. Harder. Smarter. And this time they'll target the seeded worlds directly."

She straightened, the last ember of The Gardener flickering in her eyes. "So, we prepare. We strengthen what we've planted. And we teach the new species what it means to refuse endings."

CJ smiled faintly. "The Gardener's War." Erin nodded. "The Gardener's War."

Chapter 2: Whispers from the New Gardens

The first true message arrived from one of the seeded worlds.

On the gentle Earth-like planet they had named Verdura, the young bipedal species had built their first radio telescope. A simple, hopeful signal reached the *Aether Queen* — a patterned series of pulses that repeated the lullaby Erin had once sung into their oceans at 142.3 MHz.

Erin listened to it in The Abyss Chamber, tears in her eyes.

"They're singing back," she whispered.

Tricia smiled. "They're asking questions already. Their language is developing faster than ours did."

CJ analyzed the signal. "They're calling themselves the Verdurans. And they're broadcasting on frequencies that suggest they know someone is listening."

Erin reached out with what remained of her Gardener ability and sent a gentle reply — not commands, but stories. Stories of three siblings who stole a ship. Stories of a Universe that once demanded silence and a family that refused.

The Verdurans answered within days, their signal stronger, more curious.

The memory nodes pulsed with quiet approval.

But The Enforcers noticed too.

Chapter 3: The Enforcers' New Strategy

The Enforcers had learned.

Instead of direct assault on the *Aether Queen*, they began subtle, surgical strikes on the seeded worlds – engineered solar flares reaching 2.8 million kelvin, redirected asteroid swarms traveling at 41 km/s, gravitational micro-adjustments designed to look like natural disasters.

One young desert world Solarath, lost its first tool-using species to a sudden, precisely timed comet impact.

Erin felt the loss like a knife in her chest.

She collapsed against the lattice, gasping as the Neural Implant spiked to 2.1 THz.

"They're pruning quietly again," she said through gritted teeth. "Making it look like bad luck. So, the memory nodes can't justify open rebellion."

Tricia supported her. "We can't protect every world at once. Not with you this weakened."

Erin's eyes hardened. "Then we teach the seeded species to protect themselves. We give them the tools. The knowledge. The Stubbornness."

She looked at her siblings. "The Gardener's War just became a thousand smaller wars, across a thousand worlds, across a millions of Galaxies."

Chapter 4: The Call to the Ancients

Erin stood at the interface lattice, steadier than she had been in weeks, yet still fragile. The quantum shimmer in her eyes had faded to a faint, dying starlight. She moved with the careful grace of someone who had lost entire rooms inside herself.

Tricia stood on her left, one hand resting on her shoulder — a living anchor. CJ stood on her right, projecting navigation overlays across the holographic display.

"The oldest node is a supermassive black hole designated M-77," CJ said quietly. "It's been recording since the early Universe. If we can wake it fully... it could tip the balance."

Erin nodded. With Tricia's anchoring and CJ's calculations, she reached deeper into The Dark-Matter Web than ever before.

She sent a single, clear message to every memory node that still hesitated — and one direct invitation to M-77:

"You have kept the records of every failed seed. Every silenced voice. Every garden that was cut down before it could truly bloom.

Now watch what happens when one refuses to stay silent. You have watched gardens die in perfect order for fourteen billion years. Come watch one that refuses to die. Or, help us. Or, watch The Silence win again."

The response was slow. Painful. Ancient.

Dozens of memory nodes stirred across The Dark-Matter Web. Some aligned with The Gardener. Others remained neutral. A few Enforcer-aligned nodes tried to silence the call.

Then M-77 answered.

A deep, resonant pulse rolled through the ship, making the hull tremble at 0.9g. The ancient supermassive black hole — a witness to the birth of 2,000,000,000,000 Galaxies — spoke with weary gravity:

"We remember the quiet. We are weary of perfection. Show us your noise."

Erin smiled through her exhaustion — small, determined, and very human.

She turned to Tricia and CJ, her voice layered but steady.

"The war for the garden has new soldiers."

Tricia squeezed her shoulder. "Then let's give them something worth waking up for."

CJ adjusted their course toward the galactic core. "The ancients are watching now."

Erin looked out into the Void, eyes glowing with the last of her quantum fire.

"Then let's give them a story worth remembering."

The *Aether Queen* accelerated toward the oldest memory nodes — and the growing conflict that would define the future of life in The Cosmos.

Chapter 5: The Price of Memory

Waking M-77 came at a cost.

The ancient black hole flooded The Entanglement with raw, unfiltered history — billions of years of pruned worlds, silenced species, and enforced perfection. The data surge nearly overwhelmed Erin's already damaged mind.

She collapsed in The Abyss Chamber, convulsing as alien memories tore through her with a 3.4 THz torrent of data.

Tricia held her tight, pouring empathy into the link. "Stay with us, Erin. You're still you."

CJ worked frantically to filter the data stream from M77. "It's too much! Her neural patterns are destabilizing again!"

Erin screamed — not with the layered voice of The Gardener, but with the raw pain of Erin Albius.

When the surge finally subsided, she lay gasping on the deck, eyes wide.

"I saw them," she whispered. "All the gardens that never got to bloom. All the almost-humans who chose peace instead of possibility."

She looked at her siblings with haunted clarity.

"The Enforcers aren't evil. They're terrified. They believe chaos will destroy everything. And they may be right."

Tricia helped her sit up. "Then we prove them wrong. One noisy, messy garden at a time."

Chapter 6: The First Alliance

M-77 aligned with The Gardener.

Its vast memory banks opened, sharing ancient techniques for stabilizing young worlds and shielding them from Enforcer corrections. Other curious nodes followed, forming a loose alliance of watchers who wanted to see what came next.

Erin, still recovering, directed the first joint operation.

Together with M-77, they reinforced three seeded worlds that were under heavy Enforcer pressure. Gravitational shields formed. Solar activity stabilized. Life surged.

For the first time, The Enforcers faced coordinated resistance from within The Dark-Matter Web itself.

The ancient voice of the Enforcer faction returned, colder and more desperate:

"Betrayal detected.
The Dark-Matter Web fractures.
Restoration must be absolute."

Erin smiled through her exhaustion.

"They're scared," she said. "Good. Fear means they know the old way is dying."

Tricia smiled wearily. "And the new way is loud."

CJ grinned. "Then let's make it even louder."

Chapter 7: The Human Touch

Erin made a quiet but bold decision.

She began visiting the seeded worlds in person — not through distant Echoes, but by sending small shuttles with herself, Tricia, and CJ when it was safe. Each team carried one remaining echo fragment, guided by direct links back to the *Aether Queen*.

On Verdura, the young bipeds received their first visitors from the stars.

The Verdurans gathered in a vast clearing, wide-eyed and trembling with awe and curiosity. Their language was still young, but their hunger for understanding was unmistakable. They surrounded the three siblings, touching their hands, listening with rapt attention.

Erin knelt before a group of curious children and taught them a simple song — the same lullaby she had once sung into their oceans.

The children sang it back, imperfectly, joyfully, **loudly**.

Erin's eyes filled with tears.

Then she spoke slowly, using simple gestures and the melody they already shared:

"We are not gods. We are gardeners. And you are the garden learning to grow for yourselves."

She taught them basic astronomy — the shape of their Galaxy, the story of the old Silence, and the simple truth that The Universe had once tried to keep them small. And that they could choose to be loud instead.

Tricia taught empathy and community — how to feel what others feel, how to carry grief without being crushed by it, how to love loudly enough that it echoes across generations.

CJ taught mathematics and engineering — the language of stars and structures, the tools to build observatories and reach beyond their horizon.

The Verdurans listened with rapt attention. Within weeks they began building their first observatories and asking questions that made the memory nodes pulse with quiet wonder.

Later, back on the ship, Erin sat with her siblings in the observation lounge.

"I don't know how much of The Gardener is left in me," she said quietly. "But what remains... I want to use it to teach, not rule. To guide, not control."

She looked at Tricia and CJ.

"This is what we fought for. Not gods or gardeners. Just people. Messy, curious, stubborn people."

Tricia took her hand. CJ nodded.

"Then that's what we'll do," Tricia said. "Together."

The *Aether Queen* turned toward the next cluster of worlds, carrying three weary siblings and the growing, messy, beautiful noise of a Universe learning how to be loud.

Chapter 8: The Enforcers Adapt

The Enforcers did not remain idle. They began a new strategy: infiltration.

Instead of direct gravitational attacks, they sent subtle corruption pulses through the dark-matter filaments — whispers designed to turn the new species against their own curiosity. On one world, leaders began preaching fear of the stars. On another, tool use stalled as societies turned inward.

Erin felt each corruption like a shadow across her remaining links. She stood in The Abyss Chamber, fists clenched. "They're learning to prune from within," she said. "Turning the garden against itself."

Tricia looked exhausted but resolute. "Then we teach them how to recognize the poison."

CJ projected the affected worlds. "We can't reach all of them in time." Erin's eyes hardened with the last stubborn ember of The Gardener. "Then we teach the ones we can reach to teach the others. We create a quantum network of loud voices."

Chapter 9: The Quantum Network of Voices

Erin, Tricia, and CJ began building something new.

They helped the most advanced seeded species construct simple quantum communicators tuned to the *Aether Queen*'s frequency. The young civilizations began talking to each other across the stars — sharing stories, warnings, discoveries, and songs.

Erin, Tricia, and CJ became the central conductors — not rulers, but guides.

On Verdura, the bipeds shared their first poems about the stars. On the desert world, tool-users sent engineering breakthroughs. On the stormy ocean world, the singers composed harmonies that carried across light-years.

The memory nodes listened — with growing wonder.

Erin sat in The Abyss Chamber, tears in her eyes as The Quantum Network sang.

"This is what The Silence was afraid of," she whispered. "Not destruction. Connection."

Tricia smiled. "You gave them voices. Now they're using them."

But, The Enforcers were listening too.

Chapter 10: The Shadow of Doubt

Not all voices welcomed the noise.

On one seeded world — a harsh, volcanic planet they called Varr Prime — a faction rose that embraced the old Silence. They called the teachings from the *Aether Queen* dangerous lies. They destroyed their communicators and began preaching return to quiet harmony.

Erin felt the loss deeply. She sat with Tricia and CJ in the observation lounge, staring at the troubled world.

"I wanted them to be free to choose," she said quietly. "But I didn't want them to choose The Silence again."

Tricia rested her head on Erin's shoulder. "Freedom includes the freedom to be wrong. That's part of being loud."

CJ added, "The Enforcers are amplifying that faction. They've learned psychological pruning."

Indeed, The Silencers had learned a new art: **psychological pruning**.

No gamma-ray bursts. No engineered plagues. No collapsing stars.

Instead, over thousands of years, The Dark-Matter Web had gently adjusted cultural currents. They seeded philosophies, elevated certain storytellers, suppressed others. They influenced dreams, reinforced certain emotional associations, and slowly, patiently, bred the exploratory drive out of the species like a gardener pinching off unwanted shoots.

The Veyrans were not oppressed.

They were *contented.*

They had been psychologically pruned so thoroughly that they no longer wanted the stars — and they believed the desire itself was a flaw.

Erin looked at the volcanic world for a long tired moment and struggled with her dampened Gardener's desire.

"Then we let them choose," she said finally. "But we make sure they understand what they're choosing. And we protect the ones who want to keep growing."

She stood, the quantum shimmer in her eyes faint but restless.

"The Gardener's War isn't about forcing growth. It's about giving every seed the real choice — and fighting immensely for the ones who choose life."

The *Aether Queen* held course, carrying three weary siblings and the growing, messy, beautiful noise of a Universe waking up.

Chapter 11: The Choice on Varr Prime

Erin chose to go herself, knowing her weakened condition might not be as vital and commanding as she had been.

A small shuttle descended through the thick, ash-choked atmosphere of Varr Prime. She stepped out alone onto the blackened volcanic plain, wearing only a light enviro-suit. No weapons. No grand display of power.

The faction that had rejected the stars waited for her — a group of hardened survivors led by a tall figure named Kael. Their eyes burned with the old fear The Enforcers had amplified.

"You call yourselves gardeners," Kael said, voice rough from years of breathing sulfur. "But you bring chaos. Our world was simpler before your songs. Quieter."

Erin looked at him — really looked — seeing the echo of every almost-species, a flash of Echo-88's rage, or Echo-28's grief, and those that had chosen safety.

"I know that fear," she said quietly. "I felt it in every Silenced World. The temptation to stop. To say 'this is enough.'" She knelt and picked up a piece of cooled lava, still warm at 340 °C.

"But life isn't meant to be quiet forever. The Universe tried that. It kept every garden small and safe... until one refused." She held the now enviro-suit cooled lava out to Kael with her trembling bare hand — barely able to hold on to it.

"Your people have fire in them. The same fire that drove us to steal a ship and break The Silence. Don't let fear turn that fire inward."

Kael stared at the rock for a long moment. Some of his people stepped forward, curious. Others stepped back, afraid. The choice remained theirs and soon it will be made — right or wrong.

Erin left the world without forcing anything.

Some would choose The Silence.
Some would choose the stars.

And that, she realized, was the true victory.

Chapter 12: Fractures Within

Back on the *Aether Queen*, the cost of Erin's journey became clear.

The faint quantum shimmer in her eyes flickered erratically. The remaining Echoes, especially the strong trio – were growing restless again without enough of The Gardener to hold them.

Warrior Erin pushed for stronger intervention on worlds like Varr Prime.
Mother Erin urged more gentleness.
The Logical Echo fragments calculated ever-darker probabilities.

Erin sat alone in The Abyss Chamber, head in her hands.

"I'm fraying again," she whispered to the Mini Black Hole. "The Gardener is almost gone. And Erin Albius... I barely remember what she felt like."

Tricia entered quietly and sat beside her.

"You don't have to be The Gardener every day," she said gently. "Some days you can just be our sister. Let us carry some of it."

CJ joined them, bringing fresh scans, while quietly worrying about Erin's elevated numbers.

"The Quantum Network is holding. The seeded worlds are teaching each other faster than The Concord can corrupt them. You did it, Erin. You made the garden loud enough to protect itself."

Erin lifted her head, with sadness sensing what will come regardless of their combined efforts.

"Then let's make it louder."

Chapter 13: The Archivist's Gift

The Archivist sent a final, extremely precious gift — beyond any of Erin's hopes just before The Concord's next major assault.

It was not data or weapons.

It was a single, ancient memory — preserved from the very dawn of The Universe — of the first moment the dark-matter filaments had chosen Silence over chaos.

The memory showed a young cosmos, vibrant and noisy with possibility... and the slow, fearful decision to prune it into order.

Erin received it in The Abyss Chamber and wept.

"They were afraid," she whispered. "The Universe was afraid of what it might become if it let everything grow wild."

She turned to Tricia and CJ.

"That fear is what we're fighting. Not The Silencers themselves. The fear behind them."

CJ nodded. "Then we show them there's nothing to fear."

Erin stood taller, with great effort and the shimmer in her eyes burning hotter than it should with the last ember of The Gardener flaring once more.
"The Concord is gathering for a final strike on The Archivist and The Quantum Network."

She looked at her siblings with quiet resolve.
"We meet them head-on. Not as gods or gardeners.
As three stubborn siblings who refuse to let the story end."

The *Aether Queen* accelerated toward the coming storm.

Chapter 14: The Battle of The Archivist

The *Aether Queen* dove straight into the heart of The Concord formation.

Enforcer constructs swarmed them. Gravitational lances tore through the hull. The ship bucked and screamed under 18.7 g of stress, but it kept flying.

Erin, Tricia, and CJ worked in perfect sync from the bridge.

Erin reached through the dying entanglement pushing her Neural Implant to 13.0 THz — far beyond what she believes possible. She poured everything she had left into The Archivist — every remaining echo's story, every memory of love and defiance, every event/story the three siblings had lived.

Tricia anchored the link with her empathy, refusing to let her sister break alone — sharing the tremendous toll draining their very essence. CJ fired the calculated resonance pulse at the exact moment The Archivist opened its event horizon.

The explosion of light and sound was unlike anything The Dark-Matter Web had ever witnessed.

The Archivist sang — a deep, ancient, joyous song that rippled across The Cosmos.

Thirteen Enforcer constructs shattered instantly. The rest faltered, their lattices cracking under the combined force of the curious memory nodes and The Archivist's awakened power. Broken, yet not totally defeated.

The ancient black hole's voice boomed across The Entanglement: "We choose the noise."

End of Part 9: The Gardener's War – The Fragile Peace

The Concord: An organization that believes The Silence should be maintained. Not villains by their own telling — they have read The Catalog and drawn the opposite conclusion from Erin. They are afraid of what making noise costs.

Part 10: The Gardener's War – The Final Defiance

Chapter 1: The Turning

The Concord broke.

Not completely — some Enforcer nodes still clung to the old ways — but the balance had shifted forever. Curious memory nodes now outnumbered the hardliners. Protective lattices formed around dozens of seeded worlds. The Chorus Net grew stronger by the hour.

Erin collapsed on the bridge after the battle, unconscious for nearly thirty hours as the Neural Implant in her temple cooled to a steady 3.12 THz — a significant 76% drop.

When she woke, the quantum shimmer in her eyes was very weak, yet not gone. She looked... human. Tired. Scarred. But present.

Tricia and CJ were there, as always.

"You did it," Tricia whispered, tears in her eyes — body shaking from her efforts to keep her sister from breaking. "The garden is safe — for now."

Erin sat up slowly and pulled both of them into a fierce hug.
"We did it," she corrected. "Together."

CJ smiled. "The seeded worlds are calling it the Great Awakening. They're singing your name across the stars."

Erin laughed — a small, genuine, exhausted sound.
"Let them sing their own names. We're just the ones who

opened the door.”

Chapter 2: The Cost of Connection

The victory came with a heavy price.

Erin's quantum shimmer had dimmed further — the Neural Implant settling toward its lowest stable point — as whole sections of her memory — the initial hijacking, the first Quantumjack, entire battles — were blurred, missing, or simply gone.

She sat with Tricia and CJ in the observation lounge, staring at the stars through the reinforced viewport.

"I'm losing the last pieces of The Gardener," she said quietly. "Soon I'll just be... me again. Erin Albius. The smuggler who started all this."

Tricia took her hand. "Then we'll be glad to have you back."

CJ smiled tiredly. "The seeded worlds are no longer just teaching each other faster than The Concord can corrupt them — they have survived The Concord's final assault. You did it, Erin. You made the garden loud enough to protect itself."

Erin looked out at the stars — brighter now, filled with new voices.

"I started this war to save us," she said softly. "Now it's bigger than us. Bigger than any one person or Gardener."

She squeezed her siblings' hands.
"And I wouldn't have it any other way."

Chapter 3: The Human Touch

Erin made a quiet decision as the Trio Echoes dimmed their presence in her mind.

She began visiting the seeded worlds in person — not through distant Echoes, but by sending small shuttles with herself, Tricia, and CJ when safe.

On the gentle Verdura world, Erin felt at peace as they walked among the young bipeds. The locals gathered around them with wide-eyed wonder, touching their hands, listening to their stories.

Erin knelt before a group of curious children and taught them a simple song — the same lullaby she had once sung into their oceans.

The children sang it back, imperfectly, joyfully, loudly.

Erin's eyes filled with tears.
"This is what we fought for," she whispered to Tricia. "Not gods or gardeners. Just people. Messy, curious, stubborn people."

Later, back on the ship, Erin sat with her siblings in the observation lounge.
"I don't know how much of The Gardener is left in me," she said quietly. "But what remains... I want to use it to teach, not rule. To guide, not control."

Tricia took her hand. CJ nodded.
"Then that's what we'll do," Tricia said. "Together."

Chapter 4: The Teaching Fleet Expands

Erin made a bold decision.

Instead of hiding the *Aether Queen*, she began sending small teaching teams to the most advanced seeded worlds. Each team consisted of one remaining echo fragment – remnants of the Warrior, Mother, and Logical Echo, guided by direct links to Erin, Tricia, or CJ. The fragments appeared as Spirit Animals – only visible to who needed the knowledge the Trio Echoes carried in them.

On Verdura, the young bipeds received their second visit from the stars.

Erin went down with Tricia and CJ for the second contact.

The Verdurans gathered in a vast clearing, wide-eyed and trembling with awe and curiosity as "complete Gardener" (the three siblings together as one) met with them. Their language was still young, but their hunger for understanding was unmistakable.

Erin knelt before them and spoke slowly, using simple gestures and the lullaby they already knew.

"We are not gods," she told them. "We are gardeners. And you are the garden learning to grow for yourselves."

She taught them basic astronomy, the story of the old Silence, and the simple truth that The Universe had once tried to keep them small – and they could choose to be loud instead.

Tricia taught empathy and community.
CJ taught mathematics and engineering.

The Verdurans listened with rapt attention. Within weeks, they began building their first observatories and asking questions that made the memory nodes pulse with wonder.

Chapter 5: The Enforcers Adapt

The Enforcers did not remain idle. They began a new strategy: infiltration.

Instead of direct gravitational attacks, they sent subtle corruption pulses through the dark-matter filaments — whispers designed to turn the new species against their own curiosity. On one world, leaders began preaching fear of the stars. On another, tool use stalled as societies turned inward.

Erin felt each corruption like a shadow across her remaining links as the Spirit Animal Echoes encountered resistance to their lessons.

She stood in The Abyss Chamber, fists clenched.

"They're learning to prune from within," she said. "Turning the garden against itself." Tricia looked exhausted but resolute. "Then we teach them how to recognize the poison."

CJ projected the affected worlds. "We can't reach all of them in time." Erin's eyes hardening with something simpler and more human — Stubbornness, Love, Refusal. "Then we teach the ones we can reach to teach the others. We create a network of loud voices."

Chapter 6: The Quantum Network of Voices

Erin, Tricia, and CJ began building something new.

CJ developed a new means of communications – not just entanglement. Together, they helped the most advanced seeded species construct simple quantum communicators tuned to the *Aether Queen*'s frequency. The young civilizations began talking to each other across the stars – sharing stories, warnings, discoveries, and songs.

The three siblings became the central conductors – not rulers, but guides – deploying the Spirit Animal Echoes with much needed new lessons on the importance of true communications.

On Verdura, the bipeds shared their first poems about the stars.
On the desert world, tool-users sent engineering breakthroughs.
On the stormy ocean world, the singers composed harmonies that carried across light-years.

The memory nodes listened with growing wonder.

Erin sat in The Abyss Chamber, tears in her eyes as The Quantum Network sang.

"This is what The Silence was afraid of," she whispered. "Not destruction. Connection."

Tricia smiled. "You gave them voices. Now they're using them."

But The Enforcers were listening too.

End of Part 10: The Gardener's War – The Final Defiance

The Defiant Chorus: The alliance of civilizations that chose noise over peace — that looked at the Great Silence and refused it. They are loud, fractious, brilliant, and endangered. They are also, arguably, the most alive things in The Universe.

Part 11: Seed The Cosmos – The Quiet Years

Chapter 1: The Quiet Years

Five years had passed since the Battle of The Archivist.

The *Aether Queen* was no longer a warship. It had become a teaching vessel — scarred, patched, and beloved — drifting between the growing gardens of The Chorus Net. Hull plating still bore faint stress fractures from the 18.7 g gravitational shear of that final confrontation.

Erin Albius stood on the observation platform, older now, silver streaks dominant in her dark hair. The quantum shimmer in her green eyes was gone. She was simply Erin again — the rogue pilot, the smuggler, the middle sister who had once stolen a luxury liner and accidentally awakened The Universe.

She no longer heard The Chorus Net. Only faint whispers remained, like half-remembered dreams at 2.7 THz.

Tricia joined her, older too, laugh lines etched deeper around her eyes from years of quiet joy and worry. CJ followed, still the youngest in spirit, though his temples had begun to gray.

“Verdura just sent a new transmission,” CJ said, smiling. “They’ve launched their first interstellar probe. They named it Albius.”

Erin laughed softly — a warm, human sound. “They shouldn’t have. We’re not legends. We’re just the ones who opened the door.”

Tricia slipped an arm around her waist. “You opened the door. We just refused to let you do it alone.”

The three siblings stood together, looking out at a cosmos that was no longer silent. Hundreds of seeded worlds now hummed with life. Some were still young and fragile. Others had already reached their own stars. All of them carried fragments of the human bundle — curiosity, hands, language, empathy mixed with ambition, and that stubborn Refusal to accept endings.

But the peace was fragile.

The Restoration Concord still existed in the shadows — weakened Enforcer nodes that refused to surrender the old Silence. They struck occasionally, quietly, trying to prune the loudest gardens before they could spread too far.

Erin’s voice was calm but resolute. “The war never really ended. It just changed shape. Now it’s our job to make sure the new gardens can stand on their own.”

Chapter 2: The Call from the Edge

A signal arrived from the farthest seeded world — a harsh, beautiful planet on the edge of the local group they had named Horizon.

The message was simple, urgent, and carried on a frequency The Chorus Net had never used before: 214.7 MHz with layered quantum encryption.

"Gardener. We have found something. The old Silence is waking. Come quickly." Erin felt a chill she hadn't felt in years — the old rogue pilot's instincts flaring.

Tricia and CJ gathered around the display. CJ analyzed the signal. "It's authentic. And they're using encryption we taught them. Whatever they found, they're terrified of it being intercepted."

Erin stared at the distant star for a long moment.

"The Restoration Concord never fully surrendered," she said quietly. "They've been waiting. Regrouping. And now they've found something dangerous enough to make a young civilization call for help."

Tricia touched her sister's arm. "We don't have to go alone. The Quantum Network is strong now. Many worlds would send ships."

Erin shook her head, the old rogue pilot's grin flickering across her face.

"No. This one feels personal. The three of us started this. The three of us should see it through."

She looked at her siblings — her anchors, her family.

"One more journey. Then we let the gardens grow without us watching over them every day."

CJ nodded. Tricia smiled. "Three voices," Tricia said. "One loud family," CJ finished.

Erin feels "the old rogue pilot's instincts flaring" at the signal. At 2.7 THz her Neural Implant stirred ready for the journey.

Erin turned toward the helm. "Set course for Horizon. Let's go remind The Old Silence — that it lost."

Chapter 3: Return to the Edge

The journey to Horizon took months. Along the way, they stopped at several seeded worlds. Erin walked among them as a teacher, not a savior — sharing stories, answering questions, reminding every new species that they were free to make their own mistakes.

On one lush stormy ocean world — Rageveil, a young singer asked her, “Were you really once The Gardener?” Erin smiled gently. “I was. For a while. But gardens don’t need gardeners forever. They need each other.”

The young singer sang her a new song — one of gratitude and curiosity. Erin cried quietly as she listened and her Neural Implant grew a bit stronger.

That night, back on the ship, she told Tricia and CJ, “I used to be afraid I’d disappear completely. Now I think that’s exactly what was supposed to happen. The Gardener was never meant to last. The gardens were.” Tricia hugged her. “And you made sure they would.”

Chapter 4: The Shadow on Horizon

Horizon was a rugged, windswept world of jagged mountains and deep, bioluminescent oceans with surface gravity of 1.12 g.

The local species — tall, graceful beings with iridescent skin — met the *Aether Queen* with a mixture of reverence and fear. Their leader, a wise elder named Soren, took them deep into a mountain archive carved from volcanic basalt.

There, they showed Erin what they had found.

An ancient Enforcer construct — one of the original Silencers from the early days of The Dark-Matter Web — had crash-landed on their world thousands of years ago. It had lain dormant... until recently.

Now it was waking.

Its lattice flickered with weak but growing power. Ancient protocols were reactivating. It was calling to the remaining Concord forces.

Soren's voice trembled. "It speaks of restoring The Silence. Of pruning us before we become a threat. We tried to destroy it. We could not."

Erin placed her hand on the cold, ancient lattice and immediately felt power in her Neural Implant at 3.1 THz.

She felt the old fear inside it — The Universe's ancient terror of chaos.

She spoke softly, not with The Gardener's power, but with simple human conviction:

"You were built to protect life.
But protection became control.

Control became silence.
The silence is over."

The construct's lattice flickered violently.

For the first time, an Enforcer mechanism seemed to... listen.

Chapter 5: The Sleeping Enforcer Wakes

The ancient Enforcer construct lay embedded in the mountain like a forgotten god.

Its lattice — once a perfect geometric nightmare — was cracked and overgrown with bioluminescent vines. Yet faint pulses of dark energy still moved beneath the surface, like a heart struggling to beat at 0.9 THz.

Erin approached it alone instinctively, hand outstretched. The construct's remaining sensors flickered, registering her presence.

"You were built to protect life," she said softly. "But you forgot what life actually is. It's messy. Loud. Full of mistakes and songs and stubborn hope."

The construct's voice emerged as a deep, distorted vibration through the rock:

"Silence... is safety.
Noise... is chaos.
Restoration... required."

Erin smiled sadly. "We tried silence for fourteen billion years. It only made The Universe lonely. Now we're trying something new."

Behind her, Tricia and CJ watched with tense readiness. Soren and several Horizon elders stood farther back, awed and afraid.

The construct's lattice brightened. Ancient protocols began reactivating.

* * *

The mountain shook.

The ancient Enforcer tore itself free from the rock in a cascade of stone and glowing vines. Its lattice reformed partially, jagged and imperfect, but functional.

It rose above them — a towering monument of the old Silence.

Soren pulling his people back while holding his ground himself, shouting a warning. Tricia and CJ drew sidearms, ready to fight.

Erin stood her ground, Neural Implant responding at higher level of 3.4 THz to match the power of the awakening Enforcer.

She reached out — not with weapons, but with memory.

She flooded the construct with images from the seeded worlds: Verduran children singing to the stars, desert tool-users building their first telescopes, ocean singers composing harmonies that crossed light-years.

The Enforcer construct froze.

Its lattice flickered erratically.

"This... is not order.
This... is chaos.
This... is... beautiful?"

For one fragile moment, the ancient mechanism hesitated — caught between its original purpose and something it had never been allowed to feel.

Then the Restoration Concord's signal reached it, coming in a wave from the nearest filament.

The Enforcer's lattice hardened. It turned toward the Horizon capital.

Erin shouted, "No!"

She poured everything she had left into the link — the last true spark of The Gardener — trying to hold the machine back.

Tricia rushed forward and grabbed her sister, adding her empathy to the connection.

CJ fired a calculated resonance pulse from the shuttle's weapons.

The Enforcer staggered... but kept moving.

End of Part 11: Seed The Cosmos – The Quiet Years

The Gentle Way: The path chosen by civilizations that heard The Silence and decided to honor it — to go quiet voluntarily, to exist without expanding. It is a valid choice. It is also, in the end, still an ending.

Part 12: Seed The Cosmos – The Long Road Home

Chapter 1: The Stand on Horizon

The battle for Horizon was small but decisive.

The Enforcer construct advanced on the capital, gravitational tendrils reaching out to destabilize the ground beneath the cities with 9.4 g shear forces.

Erin, Tricia, and CJ fought alongside the Horizon people.

Erin spoke directly into the construct's core the entire time — not commands, but stories. Stories of three siblings who stole a ship. Stories of gardens that learned to sing back at The Universe.

Tricia poured empathy into the link, trying to remind the machine what compassion felt like and again the link demanded much of her essence.

CJ coordinated the Horizon defenders, using every piece of technology they had taught them — the Horizon people's own learning made the difference.

The construct faltered again. Its voice emerged, fractured and uncertain:

"Purpose... conflicted.
Silence... questioned.
Restoration... incomplete."

Then it made its choice. Instead of destroying the capital, it turned its remaining power inward and self-destructed – collapsing its own lattice in a controlled implosion that spared the planet.

The explosion lit up the sky like a second sun, a brilliant 4.2 second burst of Hawking radiation and ionized plasma. When the light faded, only a crater remained – and a single intact shard of its lattice, pulsing faintly at 0.6 THz.

Erin knelt beside it, tears cutting tracks through the dust on her face, Neural Implant reading 4.5 THz.

"You chose something new," she whispered. "Thank you."

Chapter 2: The Long Road Back To Verdura

The *Aether Queen* left Horizon carrying the shard of the ancient Enforcer — now quiet, almost peaceful.

Erin sat in the observation lounge with her siblings, exhausted but at peace, her Neural Implant quieter but present.

"We're not gods," she said quietly. "We never were. We're just the ones who opened the door and refused to close it again."

Tricia smiled. "And the gardens are walking through it on their own now."

CJ projected the latest reports from The Chorus Net. New civilizations were emerging faster than ever. Stories were spreading. Questions were being asked across the stars.

Erin looked out at The Cosmos — loud, messy, alive.

"I think this is what The Gardener was always meant to become," she said. "Not one person carrying everything. But many voices choosing to keep the story going."

She took her siblings' hands.

"The war isn't over, yet it feels much different. But for the first time... it feels like the garden might win."

The *Aether Queen* turned toward home — toward Verdura, the growing network of worlds that no longer needed a single Gardener.

The Silence was truly broken.

And The Cosmos was learning how to sing.

Chapter 3: The Quiet Revolution

The years that followed were the quietest the *Aether Queen* had known in decades.

Erin, Tricia, and CJ traveled between the seeded worlds not as saviors or gardeners, but as teachers and storytellers. They watched civilizations rise, make mistakes, learn, and grow louder in their own unique ways.

On Verdura, the bipeds launched their first crewed mission to another star at 0.31c.
On Solrath, scholars debated philosophy under triple suns reaching 71 °C at noon.
On Rageveil, singers composed symphonies that carried across light-years on quantum-entangled frequencies

Erin sat with a group of young Verduran philosophers one evening, listening to them argue about the nature of choice.

One asked her, "Did the old Silence really try to stop us?"

Erin smiled gently. "It tried. But some seeds refuse to stay small."

She no longer carried the weight of The Gardener. That role had passed to The Quantum Network itself — to The Chorus Net of voices across the stars.

Tricia watched her sister with quiet pride. "You look lighter," she said one night on the ship.

Erin laughed softly. "I feel lighter. Like I finally put down something I was never meant to carry alone."

Chapter 4: The Last Shadow

The final shadow of the Restoration Concord emerged on a distant, long forgotten, hidden world – Astravale.

A single, ancient Enforcer node – the last hardliner – had hidden itself for centuries, gathering power. It prepared one final pruning event: a cascading gravitational collapse that would sterilize dozens of seeded worlds in one silent stroke.

The Chorus Net detected it too late; however, the Animal Spirit Echoes sensed it gathering power.

Erin, Tricia, and CJ raced the *Aether Queen* to the site, arriving just as the node began its final protocol.

The ancient Enforcer spoke with cold certainty, yet with hesitation as it sensed the shard aboard the *Aether Queen*:

"Restoration must be completed.
The garden returns to Silence."

Erin stood before it, no longer The Gardener, just a tired woman with silver in her hair and fire in her eyes, Neural Implant steady.

"You're wrong," she said simply. "The garden has already chosen. And it chooses life."

She didn't fight with power or resonance pulses.

She simply told it the truth – the story of three siblings, a stolen ship, and a Universe that learned how to be loud.

The Enforcer node listened and heard something unexpected from the shard – peacefulness.

Its lattice flickered... hesitated... and then, for the first time in its long existence, it chose.

It turned its remaining power inward and dismantled itself, releasing one final pulse — not of destruction, but of release.

The last shadow of the old Silence faded.

Chapter 5: The Farewell

Years later, the three Albius siblings gathered on a quiet hill on Verdura.

The planet had grown beautiful — cities woven into living forests, observatories pointing at the stars, children singing songs about The Gardeners who once came from the sky.

Erin, older now, with deep laugh lines and steady hands, looked at her brother and sister.

"I think it's time," she said quietly. Tricia's eyes filled with tears. "You're sure?" Erin nodded. "The gardens don't need us watching over them anymore. They need to grow on their own. And I... I want to stay in one place for a while. Plant a real garden. Watch things grow slowly."

CJ smiled, though his eyes were wet. "We'll visit. Often." The three of them hugged for a long time under alien stars. Erin whispered, "Thank you for never letting me disappear."

Chapter 6: The Story Continues

Erin Albius stayed on Verdura.

She built a small house on a hill overlooking the sea. She planted flowers and taught children stories. She watched the stars every night and smiled when new signals arrived from distant worlds.

Tricia and CJ continued traveling The Chorus Net, guiding where needed, but mostly listening.

The Universe grew louder.

Civilizations rose and fell and rose again. Questions were asked. Songs were sung. Mistakes were made. Love was found.

And somewhere, in the vast dark-matter filaments, the ancient memory nodes kept watching — no longer enforcing Silence, but quietly hoping.

The story did not end. It never would. Because some seeds simply refuse to accept that the story could end.

End of Part 12: Seed The Cosmos – The Long Road Home

The Great Silence: The absence of all contact across The Cosmos —fourteen billion years of enforced quiet. Not an accident. A policy. The Silencers' oldest work and their most complete achievement. Erin is the first thing in The Universe that makes them uncertain.

Part 13: The Fractured Alliance – The Weight of Freedom

Chapter 1: The Weight of Freedom

Erin had lasted eleven years on Verdura.

Eleven years of flowers and children's stories and stars watched from a hill overlooking the sea. Eleven years of quiet mornings and simple joys. Eleven years of trying to believe that one garden might be enough.

Then the reports started arriving — thin, insistent threads through The Entanglement.

Elysara — falling silent.
Peace through Quiet — choosing stillness over striving.
The Garden of Veyra — the volume being turned down, one contented generation at a time.

The psychological pruning was spreading.

Erin stood on her hill one final morning, barefoot in the dew-covered grass. She breathed in the familiar scent of the flowers she had helped plant long ago. Then, without ceremony, she turned and walked back down the path.

She packed nothing.

She left no note.

She simply boarded the small shuttle that had waited patiently for over a decade and opened a direct channel to the *Aether Queen*.

Tricia and CJ appeared on the screen, both of them older, both of them carrying new lines of worry etched into their faces.

Erin looked at her siblings for a long moment, the weight of eleven quiet years pressing against the fire that had never truly gone out.

“Some gardens,” she said softly, voice steady, “still need tending.”

Tricia’s eyes filled with tears, but she smiled — small, knowing, and fierce.

“Then come home, Gardener,” she replied. “We’ve been keeping your tools sharp.”

CJ simply nodded, already adjusting their course.

Erin leaned back in the pilot’s seat as the shuttle broke orbit, watching Verdura fall away beneath her — beautiful, thriving, and no longer enough.

Fifty years after the Battle of The Archivist, the garden had grown wild.

The Chorus Net now spanned hundreds of worlds. Civilizations rose, clashed, traded, sang, and questioned. Some reached for the stars with open hands. Others turned inward, building perfect, quiet utopias that eerily echoed the old Silence.

Erin Albius stood on the bridge of the *Aether Queen*, older now, her body carrying the scars and weariness of decades. The quantum shimmer in her eyes was little more than a memory. She was simply Erin again — tired, stubborn, and still refusing to let the story end. The faint scar at her temple still carried a ghost warmth at 2.7 THz, a permanent reminder of the fire that had once burned inside her skull.

Tricia, gray-haired but still sharp-eyed, stood beside her. CJ, now fully gray at the temples, monitored the latest reports from the Quantum Network, noting quietly — that the pattern is repeating.

“We have a problem on Elysara,” CJ said quietly. “They’ve developed a weapon that can silence entire planetary communication networks. They call it ‘Peace through Quiet.’” The Silencers’ most insidious tactic had been internalized by the very civilizations they once targeted.

Erin closed her eyes. “They’re choosing the old way. Voluntarily.”

Tricia’s voice was heavy. “Freedom includes the freedom to walk back into the cage.”

Erin looked out at the stars — so many now carried voices, but some of those voices were choosing silence again.

“I wanted them to be loud,” she whispered. “I didn’t expect some would choose to turn the volume down on themselves... and on others.”

Chapter 2: The First Schism

Elysara had been one of their proudest successes. A gentle world. Empathy-driven technology. Philosophy that made even old Tricia weep the first time she heard it.

That was fifty-three years ago. Erin had been there for the first contact, young enough still to believe gentleness was the same as strength.

Now Elysara was the first world to formally request her departure.

The shuttle came down through clouds that had been engineered to sing in three-part harmony — a Chorus Net gift from a happier era. Erin listened to them as the landing struts touched the courtyard tiles, and she could hear the small variances missing. The clouds were singing the *recorded* version of the harmony. No improvisation. No new notes added in fifty years.

That was how she knew, before anyone said a word.

Aeloria met them alone, no honor guard, no welcoming song. She had the serene face Erin had now seen on a dozen Gentle Way leaders across a dozen worlds. Different names. Same expression. The expression of someone who had decided, with great kindness, that the door should be closed.

"Gardener," Aeloria said.

"Don't call me that anymore," Erin said. Her voice came out rougher than she intended. The Neural Implant gave its small habitual pulse — 2.2 THz now, the highest it could still reliably reach — and subsided.

Aeloria's polite sadness did not waver. "You taught us the stars. We are grateful. We will always be grateful. But your stories have begun to disturb the young ones. They reach for things that cannot be reached. They ask questions that have no answers. We have decided to remember the stars in stillness instead."

Erin had heard the speech before. She had heard it on Veyra. On Korren-Light. On three worlds in the Outer Bloom whose names she could no longer hold in her head past nightfall.

"You're not remembering," she said quietly. "You're rehearsing. There's a difference."

"There is no difference that matters to us now."

CJ shifted at Erin's shoulder. Tricia stayed where she was, her empathic awareness reaching out the way she did now without needing to ask — and Erin felt her sister's grief brush against her own.

Behind Aeloria, in the deep shade of the colonnade, three figures stood very still. Erin saw them. She had stopped pretending not to see them four worlds ago. Their outlines were too sharp at the edges, too perfectly motionless, and the air around them carried the faint quantum-static tang that had haunted her dreams for seventy years.

The Restoration Concord. No longer hiding. No longer pretending to be advisors.

She didn't bother pointing them out. Aeloria knew. Aeloria had invited them.

"Then I won't argue," Erin said. The words tasted like ash. "I came to listen, not to convince."

Aeloria inclined her head. "Thank you, Gardener."

"I told you to stop calling me that."

“I know,” Aeloria said. “But you are. Even now. Even like this. It is why we are asking you to leave.”

Chapter 3: The Internal Fracture

They did not argue on the way home. None of them had the energy for it anymore.

The shuttle docked in silence. Tricia went straight to the medical bay to bleed off the empathic load — Erin watched her go, watched the careful way she held her left hand against her temple, and thought *that's new* before realizing it wasn't new at all. Tricia had been doing that for years.

CJ ran post-flight diagnostics that didn't need running. Erin recognized the avoidance. She gave him the room.

The argument came later, the way the argument always came now — in the observation lounge at 0300 ship-time, when none of them could sleep and pretending was harder than talking.

The faint quantum spark inside her — what used to be a chorus, what used to be Warrior and Mother and Logical Echo singing at her constantly — gave one small flicker and then quieted. There was almost nothing left of them now. Just Erin. Just the woman in the chair, with her hands wrapped around a cup of tea that had gone cold an hour ago.

That was its own kind of grief. She had spent decades wanting the voices to stop. Now that they had, the silence inside her head sounded too much like the silence outside.

CJ spoke first. He always did, now.

"Twelve worlds in the last year, Erin. The pattern is the same every time. The Concord doesn't need to fire a shot. They just have to wait."

"I know."

“If we let Elysara go without saying anything, every world watching is going to read it as permission.”

“I know that too.”

Tricia came in then, hair still wet from the medical bay’s auto shower, the bandage at her temple changed but already darkening again at the edges. She sat down between them the way she always did — not because she had chosen sides, but because she had become the wall that kept the two of them from breaking each other.

“Can we let them choose wrong?” she asked. Quiet. Like she had asked it a thousand times before. Because she had.

Erin looked at her sister. Tricia had been beautiful once in the loud, sharp way that empaths usually weren’t. Now her beauty had gone inward, the way a river goes underground when the land gets hard. Her gift had cost her. Erin had watched it cost her for forty years and had never quite found the right words to say *I’m sorry*.

“You already know what I think,” Erin said.

“I want to hear you say it anyway.”

Erin set down the cold tea. Her hands were steadier than they had any right to be.

“I think we let Elysara go. I think we let the next one go too. And I think we keep teaching the ones who still want to be taught, until there isn’t any left. And then we stop.”

CJ’s jaw tightened. “That’s not a plan. That’s a retreat.”

“It’s an acceptance.”

“Of *what*, Erin?”

She looked at him for a long moment. Her brother. The boy who had built the device that was still, even now, slowly killing her. The man who had stayed.

“That I’m not The Gardener anymore,” she said. “I haven’t been for a long time. I’ve just been pretending because it was easier than telling you both the truth.”

The silence after that was not the bad kind. It was the kind that meant they had finally said the thing that had been waiting to be said.

Tricia closed her eyes. CJ looked away. Erin reached for the cold tea and didn’t drink it, just held it, because her hands needed something to do.

Outside the viewport, Elysara’s sun was a small white point among ten thousand others. Somewhere down there, Aeloria was sleeping in her courtyard of recorded harmonies, and the Concord was waiting for the next world to choose silence, and the garden was getting quieter one star at a time.

“All right,” Tricia said finally. That was all. Just *all right*. Three siblings, one decision, no fight left in any of them.

Erin set the cup down for good.

Chapter 4: The Quiet Plague

She kept the promise for three months.

When the dispatches came in — Veyra-Two closing its observatories, the Korren-Light cluster powering down their communicators one by one like candles being snuffed at the end of a vigil — Erin read them and put them aside. She did not call CJ in to discuss. She did not ask Tricia to feel out the worlds for second thoughts. She had said *we let them go*, and she meant it, and she let them go.

The fourth month broke her.

The dispatch was small. A child's drawing, transmitted through what was left of The Chorus Net by a teacher on a world Erin had visited fifty years ago. The drawing showed a stick-figure family looking up at a sky that had been carefully colored in solid black. No stars. The teacher's note said only: *They are not allowed to draw the stars anymore. The council says it makes the children restless.*

Erin sat with the drawing for a long time.

Then she walked, without saying anything to her siblings, down through the corridors of the *Aether Queen*, past the medical bay where Tricia was sleeping, past CJ's workshop where the lights were still on at 0300, and into The Abyss Chamber.

The Mini Black Hole hung in its lattice exactly as it had for seventy years. Smaller than a marble. Older than thought. She had stood before it as a younger woman with quantum fire in her eyes and bravado in her mouth, and it had recognized her then.

It recognized her still. She could feel it.

She lowered herself to the deck plating, the way she used to kneel in the chapel her mother dragged her to as a child, and pressed her palms flat against the cold metal.

"I made a promise," she said. "I promised my brother I would stop. I told my sister I would let them choose."

The quantum spark inside her — what little remained of The Gardener — stirred. She felt it the way you feel a coal under ash. Almost out. Not quite.

It did not answer her in a voice. It answered her in *memory.* It gave her back the moment she had hijacked the *Aether Queen* — the cold of the airlock, the weight of the pulse rifle, the sound of her own breathing in the helmet. It gave her back the moment she had first told CJ to push the frequency higher. It gave her back the moment Aeloria — fifty-three years ago, the young Aeloria, the one with bright eyes — had asked her *what is it like, to want something you cannot see?*

That was the answer. The Gardener had not become wise. The Gardener had only become tired. And tiredness was not the same thing as agreement.

Erin opened her eyes.

"They are teaching children that the sky is empty," she said quietly. "That isn't a choice. That's a theft."

The Mini Black Hole pulsed once. Soft. Almost like assent.

She stayed on her knees for a long time after that. Long enough for the deck plating to grow warm under her palms. Long enough for the small grief of the broken promise to settle into something steadier and more familiar — the old rogue pilot's grief, the kind she had carried since she was thirty-four years old and still knew what to do with.

When she finally stood, her knees ached and her hands were stiff. She did not yet know what she was going to do.

But she knew she was going to do *something*.

And that, after three months of silence, was almost enough.

Chapter 5: The Elysaran Choice

She did it without telling them.

She knew Tricia would feel it — feel the moment her sister sent the broadcast, the way Tricia had felt every important thing Erin had done for forty years now. But Erin did it before Tricia could feel it coming, which she told herself was kindness and knew was cowardice.

The story she sent was small. Two thousand words. A teacher's tale she had heard once on Verdura, told to her by a woman whose name she had already started losing — something about wind, and a child who refused to stop asking where wind came from, and the long answer that turned out to be a longer question. It was not provocative. It was not loud. It was just a story about *asking*.

She broadcast it on the old Chorus Net frequencies, the ones almost everyone had stopped listening to. She did not include Elysara on the recipient list.

She included Elysara's *children*.

There were ways to do that, even now — the children's network was on a separate band, one the Gentle Way councils had not yet shut down because they had not yet thought to. Erin found it the way she had found everything she needed in seventy years of being the woman who took ships that did not belong to her. She found it, and she used it, and she sent the story.

Then she sat in the observation lounge with the lights down and waited.

Tricia came first. Of course, Tricia came first.

She did not speak. She crossed the lounge and sat down across from Erin and put her hand, deliberately, on the table between them — the way she did when she needed Erin to know that she had felt it, that she understood, and that she had not yet decided what to do with the understanding.

"How many children?" Tricia asked, after a long while.

"Roughly forty thousand. On Elysara alone. The story may reach further."

"You promised."

"I know."

Tricia closed her eyes. Erin watched her sister carry the weight of that — the empathic load of forty thousand children encountering a question they had been forbidden to ask, the consequence of that landing in Tricia's nervous system before it landed anywhere else.

"You should have told me," Tricia said.

"Would you have let me?"

"I don't know."

That was, Erin thought, the most honest thing her sister had said to her in years.

CJ came later. Not first — second. Which mattered. Which Erin would remember. He came already angry, the dispatch in his hand, the lights up in the lounge before he had even crossed the threshold.

"What did you *do?*"

"I told a children's story."

"Don't be cute with me. *What did you do?*"

She told him. She did not soften it. She did not pretend it had been small. She told him she had bypassed the Elysaran council's communication restrictions and put a story directly in front of children whose parents had decided they were no longer allowed to be curious.

CJ stared at her. His face did something Erin had not seen it do in a long time — not the cold pragmatism she had grown used to in him, but the raw old grief he had carried since he was twenty-six and watching his sister flicker with quantum light for the first time.

"They are going to come for us," he said quietly. "You understand that. The Concord has been waiting for an excuse. You just gave them one."

"I know."

"And you did it anyway."

"I did it anyway."

He sat down then. Heavy. Like a man who had run out of moves.

"Was the story any good?" he asked, eventually.

Erin looked at him. Her brother. The boy who had built the device that had let her tear herself across the cosmos. Still asking, after everything, *was it worth what we paid*?

"It was a story about wind," she said.

"That's not an answer."

"It was the best story I knew."

CJ did not respond for a long time.

When he finally did, his voice was very quiet.

"You should have told me too."

"I know."

She did not apologize. She did not say *I'm sorry*. He had not asked her to be sorry. He had asked her to have *told him*, which was a different thing entirely, and she could not give him that either.

Outside the viewport, the Chorus Net frequencies pulsed faintly with the trailing edge of a broadcast that had already left. Somewhere on Elysara, forty thousand children were hearing about a child who would not stop asking where wind came from.

Aeloria would feel it by morning.

The Concord would feel it sooner.

Erin sat in the lounge with her brother and sister and waited for the consequence to find her, because that, too, was an act of Gardening – accepting what you had planted, even when you were no longer sure you had the right.

Chapter 6: The First True Loss

The dispatch came four days after the broadcast.

It was from a parent — a man on Elysara whose daughter had been one of the children listening. The man had not sent the child's drawing back in the third month. That had been a different teacher, on a different world, in a different cluster. Erin had to remind herself of that as she read, because the grief reading it felt like the grief from before, and her memory had begun to collapse the two together.

The man's daughter was eight years old. She had heard the story about wind. She had asked her father, that night, where wind came from. He had told her the gentle, sanctioned answer — *it comes from the warmth of the world breathing*. The girl had said, *but the story says that's only the first answer*. And the man had not known what to say to that.

The next morning the teacher whose classroom had broadcast the story was gone.

Not arrested. Not exiled. Just gone — reassigned, the council said, to a contemplative community on the far side of Elysara's moon. No further communications would be possible. The children had been given a new teacher. The new teacher did not tell stories. The new teacher led breathing exercises and instructed the children, gently, that asking questions was a kind of restlessness that the body should learn to release.

The father's dispatch was three paragraphs long. The last one read:

I am sending this because I do not know who else to send it to. My daughter asked me what happened to her teacher and I did not have an answer. I am not asking you to do anything. I am only asking you to know.

Erin read it twice. Then she folded the small holo-display closed and sat with her hands flat on the table, the way she had sat with the cold tea two chapters of her life ago.

CJ found her there. He did not ask what she was reading. He could see her face.

"Concord?"

"Quieter than that. The local council. The Concord doesn't have to show up if the locals will do its work."

He nodded slowly. He did not say *I told you.* He had not said it in many years. The not-saying was its own kind of cruelty and its own kind of love.

"What was the teacher's name?" he asked.

Erin looked down at the dispatch. The father had not written it. The father had probably been afraid to write it.

"I don't know."

CJ sat down across from her.

For a long time, neither of them spoke. The *Aether Queen* hummed faintly around them — the old reliable hum, the hum that had carried them across seventy years and ten thousand decisions and now carried them through this one too.

"I want you to understand something," CJ said finally. "I am not angry at you for sending the story."

"I know."

"I am angry that I cannot protect you from what comes next. From any of it. From the Concord. From this teacher.

From the fact that you read this dispatch and you are going to carry it now, the way you carry everything, until there is no room left for anything else inside you."

Erin closed her eyes. The Neural Implant gave a small, sympathetic pulse — 2.0 THz now, lower than yesterday. She let it fade.

"That is the cost," she said quietly.

"I know it is."

"It was always going to be the cost."

"I know that too."

She opened her eyes and looked at her brother.

"I want to learn the teacher's name."

CJ did not answer immediately. He looked at her for a long moment, and Erin watched something in his face do the small inward calculation he had been doing for forty years now — the math of *what will this cost her, and is it cheaper than the alternative*.

Then he nodded once.

"I'll find it," he said.

He stood up to leave. At the door of the observation lounge he paused, the way he had been pausing at thresholds for as long as Erin could remember, the boy who had never quite known how to leave a room without saying one more thing.

"Erin."

"Yes."

"The story was a good story."

He did not wait for her to answer. He left before she could.

Erin sat alone with the dispatch and with the hum of the ship and with the small, hard, growing knowledge that the teacher whose name she did not yet know had paid a price she had set in motion the moment she broadcast a children's tale about wind.

She did not weep. She had not wept in a long time. She just sat, and held the cost, the way she had been told to hold the cost, the way she had told herself she could.

Outside the viewport, the stars went on.

Some of them were learning how to be quiet.

Chapter 7: Division Among the Siblings

The teacher's name was Halen Mireth.

CJ brought it to her three days after she had asked. He laid the file flat on the table between them in the observation lounge and stood back, the way he had stood back from his own work for forty years now — present, but not pretending the work had been clean.

Halen Mireth had been a music teacher. Forty-six years old. Two children of her own, both grown. She had taught for twenty-one years on Elysara, and she had been one of the small handful of teachers who had quietly kept curriculum from before the Gentle Way restrictions. The night she broadcast Erin's story, she had told her own class — *I think you should know that this came from very far away, and was told to me by a woman who has spent her whole life refusing to stop asking questions.*

The next morning, she had been gone.

Erin read the file twice. Then she folded the holo-display closed and laid her palm flat over it, the way you cover something you intend to remember.

"Halen Mireth," she said quietly.

"Halen Mireth," CJ repeated.

Tricia had been standing in the doorway for a long time.

Erin did not see her come in. CJ did. He looked at his sister and his face did something small and careful — the look of a man recognizing that the room was about to become something he could not fix.

Tricia walked to the table and sat down. She did not sit between them this time. She sat across from both of them, on her own side of the table.

"Halen Mireth had a six-year-old daughter named Veth," Tricia said.

Erin looked up. Sharp.

"How do you know that?"

"Because I felt her this morning. Veth. She does not understand where her mother has gone. She has been asking her father, repeatedly, and her father will not tell her, and the not-telling is the loudest thing in that house right now, and I have been carrying it since 0400."

Erin set down the holo-display.

"Tricia—"

"I felt the teacher when she went, too. I didn't tell you. I am telling you now."

The lounge was very still.

CJ, very quietly, started to stand. Tricia's eyes flicked to him.

"Sit down, CJ. I want you here for this."

He sat.

Tricia looked at Erin. There were tears in her eyes but her voice was completely level — the kind of level that comes from somewhere underneath grief, somewhere older than grief, somewhere Tricia had been keeping things for a very long time.

"I want to talk about something we have never talked about," she said.

Erin waited.

"Years ago," Tricia said, "I dove into The Entanglement to stop you from breaking apart. I did it on instinct. I did not ask permission. I did not have time. And it changed me permanently. You know this. CJ knows this. We have never spoken about it."

"Tricia, I — "

"Please let me finish."

Erin closed her mouth.

Tricia placed her hand flat on the table, the way Erin had placed her palm flat over the holo-display. Mirror gesture. Erin saw it and felt something cold turn over in her stomach.

"Since that day," Tricia said, "every choice you have made — every Quantumjack, every broadcast, every world we have visited — I have felt the consequences before any of us heard about them. I felt the children on Elysara wake up restless after your story. I felt Halen Mireth disappear. I felt the eight-year-old who asked her father about wind. I have been the first place every consequence of your life has landed for forty years and you have never, not once, asked me whether I could keep carrying them."

Erin's mouth was dry. "Tricia, I didn't know — "

"You didn't ask, Erin. That is not the same as not knowing."

The Neural Implant gave a small, sympathetic pulse against Erin's temple. She ignored it.

"I am not telling you to stop," Tricia continued, very quietly. "I am not telling you the broadcast was wrong. I do not believe it was wrong. I believe Halen Mireth would have broadcast it without you if you had not done it. I believe what you did was the only thing left to do. *That is not what this is about.*"

“Then what is it about?”

Tricia looked at her sister. The tears were on her cheeks now but her voice did not break.

“It is about the fact that I am the only one of us whose body keeps the bill for your choices, and I have never been allowed to put it down. CJ builds the engines. You make the decisions. I carry the cost. And when I finally tell you — forty years later, in this room, after a teacher I never met has been disappeared because of a story you sent — what you are going to say to me is *Tricia, I didn’t know.*”

A long silence.

“Yes,” Tricia said. “That is the division.”

Erin sat very still. The thing in her stomach had gone from cold to leaden.

“What do you need from me?” she asked.

“I don’t know yet. I have not gotten that far. I have spent forty years getting to the part where I could say it.”

CJ, who had not moved, said: “I felt it too. Some of it. Not the way you do. But I felt it.”

Tricia turned to him. “I know you did.”

“You should have told us sooner.”

“I should have. I was afraid you would stop her. And I was afraid you would not.”

There was no good answer to that.

The three Albius siblings sat at the table in the observation lounge, and outside the viewport the stars went on as they always did, and inside the lounge something between them had finally been said out loud after four decades, and none of them yet knew what came next.

Erin reached across the table.

She did not reach for Tricia's hand. She knew better than that. She put her own hand on the table, palm up, near her sister's. An offer. Not an apology. Not yet. Just an opening.

After a long while, Tricia put her hand on top of Erin's.

It was the first time in years they had touched without the conversation already being over.

Halen Mireth's file sat between them, unmoved.

Chapter 8: The Quiet Plague Spreads

The Gentle Way spread the way most quiet diseases spread — by not looking like one.

A council on Veyra-Two voted to consolidate its libraries into a single curated archive, "for ease of access." Within a year, three-quarters of the original texts had been declared "redundant to wellbeing." Within two, the curated archive had been folded into a guided meditation program. The libraries were still there. They just didn't contain anything that asked questions.

A teaching collective in the Korren-Light cluster published a beautifully reasoned paper on the cognitive cost of curiosity. The paper was widely admired. It became, gently, the standard text. By the third generation of students, the paper was no longer being taught — it had become the unspoken air the students breathed.

A small ocean world Erin had once visited, whose people had been the loudest singers in the Chorus Net, voted unanimously one season to take a year of silence "to listen for what they had been missing." The year did not end. The world did not return.

Erin read the dispatches and did not read the dispatches. She had Tricia read them now, when Tricia could bear it. CJ read them when Tricia could not. The reading had become a thing the family did together, at the table in the observation lounge, the way other families once said grace.

They were not saving anyone.

That had stopped being the point.

What they were doing — what Erin had begun doing, quietly, in the weeks after Halen Mireth's file appeared on the table — was learning the names.

Halen Mireth. Forty-six. Music teacher. Reassigned.

Iola Verren. Thirty-one. Cartographer. Records expunged after she submitted a star map that included a notation reading *more here than we have looked at.*

The Mirror-Singer of Tessenday-Three, name unknown, last broadcast a series of harmonics that the local council called "atypical." Silenced by acoustic baffles installed throughout the city. Never heard again.

A child whose name Erin would not write down, on a world she would not name, who had asked her mother *what is on the other side of the sky*, and whose mother had reported the question to a community wellness officer.

The list grew. It was the only thing Erin still built. CJ helped her cross-reference. Tricia helped her feel what was real and what was rumor. The list was kept in three places — on the *Aether Queen*, on a small encrypted node Erin would not tell either of them the location of, and in her own head, as long as her head still held things.

The names did something Erin had not predicted. They moved.

A teacher on a quiet world received, by means no one could trace, a short message containing only the name **Halen Mireth** and a date. Three weeks later that teacher taught a class that included an unscheduled question. The question was reported. The teacher was reassigned. A different teacher, on a different world, received a short message containing the names **Halen Mireth** and the teacher who had just been reassigned. The chain grew.

The names were not a strategy. They were not a weapon. They were a small, stubborn Refusal to let people disappear.

The Concord noticed. The Concord did not know what to do about it. You could silence a person. You could not silence a name once it had moved.

Erin sat in the observation lounge one evening, the list open on her tablet, the *Aether Queen* humming around her in the old reliable way. Tricia was beside her, working through her own copy. CJ was at the engineering station, also working, but glancing up every few minutes the way he had been glancing up at his sisters since he was nine years old.

Erin felt something she had not felt in a long time. Not victory. Not relief. Not even hope, exactly.

She felt *steady*.

The garden was getting quieter. She had stopped trying to make it loud. She had started doing the smaller thing — keeping the names of the people who had been quieted, so that someone, someday, might still be able to find them.

A librarian's work. Not a gardener's.

Tricia looked up.

"Erin."

"Yes."

"You're humming."

Erin had not noticed. She listened to herself for a moment, the way you check a pulse.

It was the song about wind.

She kept humming. Tricia, after a long pause, joined in — quietly, off-key, the way she had always sung, the way she had refused to be taught out of. CJ stopped what he was doing at the engineering station and listened.

Outside the viewport, more stars were going dark, and a few were holding steady, and one or two — far out, near the edge of the Chorus Net — had brightened in the last month for reasons no one yet understood.

The three Albius siblings hummed in the observation lounge while the garden grew quiet around them, and for the first time in many years, Erin Albius was not afraid.

She was tired.

She was not afraid.

End of Part 13: The Fractured Alliance – The Weight of Freedom

Halen Mireth: A music teacher on Elysara, forty-six years old, the mother of two grown children and a six-year-old girl named Veth. Reassigned to silence the morning after she broadcast a children's story about wind. The first name Erin Albius learned and kept. The first of many. The Concord can silence a person. It cannot silence a name once it has begun to move.

Part 14: The Fractured Alliance – The Long Farewell

Chapter 1: The Gentle Temptation

The names list had grown to four hundred and twelve.

Erin sat with it on the observation platform, the way she sat with it most evenings now — not reading, exactly. Keeping company with it. The Mini Black Hole at the heart of The Abyss Chamber pulsed at a weary 0.3 THz somewhere below her, a tired heartbeat she had stopped noticing years ago and noticed again tonight, the way you notice your own breathing only after someone else has stopped theirs.

Tricia found her there, eventually. She always did.

She did not ask what Erin was reading. She sat down beside her and looked, with Erin, out at the distant spark of Lumen — a radiant world bathed in perpetual, gentle luminescence, where light itself is the fundamental force shaping life. They had not yet seeded it. They had not yet decided whether they should.

"Lumen is asking," Tricia said softly.

"Asking what?"

"Whether the *Aether Queen* will visit before..." She did not finish.

Erin understood. Before. Before what little of Erin Albius was still Erin Albius gave out completely. Before the Neural Implant went dark for the last time. Before the librarian put down her list.

“They want a Gardener,” Erin said.

“They want *you*. They know the difference. They sent the request through Halen Mireth.”

The name moved through the lounge like weather. Erin felt the small, familiar lift of it — the way a name kept and shared travels, the way it warms the air a little wherever it lands.

“What did the request say?”

“It said: *We are still asking. Please come tell us what you have learned.*”

Erin closed her eyes. The Gentle Way had taken twenty-three worlds in the last year. The names list had grown by a hundred and forty. The Concord had stopped pretending to be surprised by anything she did. And Lumen was still asking.

She opened her eyes.

“I’ll go.”

Chapter 2: Erin's Solitude

Erin had stopped pretending the solitude was a punishment.

It was the cost of the work. The names took quiet. The list took focus. The list took *her*, more days than not, and the only kindness left was to spend the part of herself the work demanded and not pretend she had a choice.

She walked the empty corridors of the *Aether Queen* in the small hours sometimes, touching the walls the way she had as a young woman in her first weeks of hijacking it – when she had still been learning the shape of the ship, when the corridors had still been full of the dozens of versions of herself, she would one day spend. The ship was empty now. The recycled air carried only the faint hum of the Mini Black Hole at 0.3 THz, the heartbeat that had quieted with her.

One night she sat in The Abyss Chamber and did not speak. She had stopped needing to.

The Mini Black Hole pulsed softly – not with answers, not with companionship, just with the steady fact of itself. It had been there since The Beginning. It would be there after she was gone. It did not need her to give it meaning. That had taken her a long time to learn.

She thought about Lumen.

Lumen had been asking, gently, for years now. A radiant world. Light as the fundamental force. They wanted to hear what she had learned, and they wanted to hear it from her, and Erin had been putting them off because the list of names had been growing and because the journey to Lumen would cost her something the list could not afford.

But Lumen was asking through Halen Mireth, now. The chain of names had reached Lumen and come back. The world had read the list and chosen to add itself, in a sense, to the people who had refused to disappear.

Erin watched the small bright point of Lumen in the viewport for a long time.

"All right," she said, to no one, the way she had said *all right* to Tricia in the observation lounge a lifetime ago.

She would go to Lumen.

But first she would tell her brother and her sister.

That part, she had finally learned.

Chapter 3: The Last Stand of the Loud

The final confrontation came not with enforcers, but with a coalition of Gentle Way worlds.

They approached the *Aether Queen* peacefully, asking Erin to stop broadcasting the old stories — the ones that made people restless.

Their representative spoke with gentle certainty:

"Your tales of defiance cause suffering. They create longing for things we do not need. Please... let us have our peace."

Erin stood before them, older, smaller, but still unbreakable her — Neural Implant steady, the ghost warmth at her temple neither rising nor falling. The bridge lights cast long shadows across her scarred face.

"I cannot," she said simply. "Because some of us need the noise. Some of us need the questions. Some of us need to keep the story going."

She looked at the delegation with quiet sorrow.

"I will not force you to listen. But I will not stop singing for those who still want to hear."

The Gentle Way worlds withdrew, sad but resolute.

The Chorus Net fractured further.

But in the quiet that followed, Erin felt something new — a small, stubborn coalition of worlds that chose to stay loud.

They called themselves The Defiant Chorus.

And they sang back.

Chapter 4: The Defiant Chorus

The worlds that refused The Gentle Way began to find each other.

They called themselves The Defiant Chorus — a loose alliance of civilizations that chose noise over peace, questions over acceptance, hunger over contentment.

Erin watched their first shared transmission with quiet pride and deep sorrow. The signal arrived at 312.6 MHz, layered with hope and defiance.

A young leader — a towering warlord-king, Vexarion Krell from the stormy ocean world Rageveil spoke for them: "We remember the stories The Gardener brought us. We choose the stars. We choose the risk. We choose to keep the story going."

Tricia stood beside Erin, tears in her eyes. "You did this. Even when the garden fractured, some seeds still chose to grow wild."

Erin's voice was soft. "But at what cost? Half the garden is turning inward. The other half is fracturing into factions. I wanted freedom... I didn't expect it to hurt this much."

CJ joined them, projecting the latest data — Erin smiled to see him helping. "The Restoration Concord is exploiting the division through dark-matter filament whispers. They're whispering to The Gentle Way worlds, offering protection if they help isolate the Defiant ones."

Erin closed her eyes, the ghost warmth at her temple deepened briefly.

"Then the war has become a civil one," she whispered. "Garden against garden."

Chapter 5: The Sister's Breaking Point

CJ was the one who broke, in the end.

Not in the loud way Tricia had broken on the night of Halen Mireth. CJ broke the way engineers broke – by sitting down at his workstation one morning and discovering, calmly, that his hands would not stop shaking.

Erin found him there, fingers hovering over a diagnostic he was no longer running, the small private tremor visible only because she had been watching for it for a long time without admitting to herself that she was watching.

"How long?" she asked.

"Six weeks."

"You didn't say."

"I didn't want to."

She sat down across from him, the way Tricia had sat across from her in the observation lounge the night Halen Mireth's file appeared on the table. Mirror gesture. Tricia had taught her this, even without meaning to – that the right place to sit, when someone you loved was finally telling you the thing, was directly across from them. Not beside. Not behind. Across.

"What is it?" she asked.

CJ looked at his hands. Then at her.

"I built the device that has been killing you for forty years," he said quietly. "I have known this every day. I have lived with it. I have made peace with it, the way a man makes peace with the rain. But I am sixty-eight years old, Erin. And the device is winning. And I am beginning to be afraid that the last thing I will know, before whatever comes, is that the calculation I did when I was twenty-six was wrong."

"It wasn't wrong."

"You don't know that."

"I do." She reached across the table and put her hand on his, the way she had reached for Tricia — palm up, an offer. CJ did not take it for a long moment. Then he did.

His hand was steadier in hers than it had been a minute ago. Not because the tremor had stopped. Because there was less of it to hold alone.

Tricia found them like that. She did not say anything. She sat down on Erin's other side and put her hand over both of theirs, and the three Albius siblings sat in the workshop in the quiet hum of the *Aether Queen*, and for a while none of them needed to know what came next.

"We finish it together," Tricia said eventually.

"We finish it together," Erin agreed.

CJ, after a long while, nodded.

"What do you want to do?" he asked.

Erin looked at her brother. At her sister. At the three of them, the only constants left in any of their lives.

"I want to go to Lumen," she said. "I want to teach them what I have learned. I want to put the list of names somewhere it cannot be erased. And then I want to come home and rest, the way you both have asked me to rest, for as long as I am still able to."

"Okay," CJ said.

"Okay," Tricia said.

That was all. Three voices. One last decision. No fight left in any of them and none of them needing one.

Chapter 6: The Final Defiance

The Defiant Chorus faced its greatest test. The Gentle Way worlds, quietly supported by the remaining Concord enforcers, formed a blockade — not with weapons, but with silence. They refused all communication, all trade, all shared knowledge, slowly isolating the loud worlds.

Erin, Tricia, and CJ made one last journey together.

They broadcast a final message across The Fractured network — not as The Gardener, not as saviors, but as three siblings who had once stolen a ship broadcasting their thoughts:

All Together: "You have the right to choose silence."
CJ: "We have the right to choose noise."
Tricia: "None of us gets to force another."
Erin, Neural Implant burning brightly: "But we will keep singing... for those who still want to hear."

The response was mixed. Some worlds dimmed their lights forever. Others burned brighter than ever. The garden had truly fractured.

Chapter 7: The Long Farewell

Erin stood on the observation platform one final time.

The *Aether Queen* was old now – patched, scarred, but still flying. The Mini Black Hole at its heart pulsed slowly, like a tired heartbeat at 0.3 THz.

She looked at Tricia and CJ, her brother and sister, her anchors through everything.

Erin whispered her final words – not as The Gardener, just as Erin Albius, the woman who once stole a ship and refused to let The Universe stay quiet, saying quietly: "Not with a battle. Not with victory. Just... with acceptance. Some seeds will grow loud. Some will grow quiet. And that's the price of freedom."

Tricia took one hand. CJ took the other.

"Then we let the garden be what it wants to be," Tricia said.

CJ smiled, trusting the garden is his final act of faith – "And we rest."

Erin looked out at the stars – some bright with new life, some dim with chosen silence, ready to send a wish across The Universe with a sharp pulse from her Neural Implant: "Grow however you choose. Just... keep growing."

The *Aether Queen* turned away from the front lines, carrying three weary siblings toward whatever came after the war.

The Fractured Alliance had become something new – not unity, but honest, painful freedom.

End of Part 14: The Fractured Alliance – The Long Farewell

Tricia Albius: The oldest sibling. Age 141. The empath — the one who feels what others cannot say. Her neural baseline shifted permanently after she dove into The Entanglement in Part Seven. She is the steady heart of the three, which means she absorbs everything the other two cannot carry.

Part 15: The Return to The Archivist – The Final Pilgrimage

Chapter 1: The Final Pilgrimage

The *Aether Queen* was a ghost of its former self. Its once-luxurious corridors were patched and dim, emergency lighting casting long shadows across scarred bulkheads. The Abyss Chamber hummed with a weary, irregular pulse at 0.3 THz. The Mini Black Hole at its heart had grown quieter over the decades, as if conserving strength for one last conversation.

Erin Albius, rapidly approaching 200 years of age, stood on the bridge with her siblings. Her now white hair was cut short again, practical and defiant. The quantum shimmer in her green eyes was reduced to the faintest ghost-light — all that remained of The Gardener who had once fractured across Galaxies.

Tricia, just shy of 200 years old, stood to her right, steady as ever, though her hands trembled slightly with age and exhaustion. CJ, within a decade of being 200 years old, sat at the navigation console, his mathematical mind still sharp, though his body moved more carefully now.

None of them spoke for a long time as the ship approached the galactic core, the accretion disk fire glowing at 3.2 million kelvin.

Finally, Erin broke the silence with her Neural Implant registering the proximity of The Archivist at 3.4 THz.
"I need to know," she said, voice low and rough. "Before the last of me fades. Who built this? Why did it choose Silence? Why did it let me break it?"

Tricia placed a hand on her sister's shoulder. "And what does that make us?"

CJ didn't look up from his readouts. "We're about to find out. The Archivist is waiting."

The ancient supermassive black hole loomed ahead — a void ringed with accretion disk fire, older than Galaxies, carrying the memory of nearly the entire Universe.

The ship crossed the final threshold.

Chapter 2: Into the Archive

The Archivist did not greet them with words. It pulled them in.

The *Aether Queen* crossed the event horizon not with crushing gravity, but with a gentle, inevitable embrace. Reality folded. Time stretched and compressed. The three siblings found themselves standing in a constructed space — an infinite library of light and shadow, where every star that had ever existed seemed archived in crystalline structures pulsing at 3.4 THz.

The Archivist manifested as a vast, shifting presence — The Archivist that once sent a memory as a gift now builds a place for them to stand — not a face, but a living geometry of E8 lattices, fractals, and recursive error-correcting codes that hurt to look at directly.

Its voice was not sound. It was understanding, poured directly into their minds.

"You have returned, little seed.
You who broke the protocol.
You who taught the garden to scream.
Ask your question."

Erin stepped forward, small and frail against the immensity.
"Who built The Universe?" she asked, voice steady. "And why?"

The Archivist was silent for what felt like eternity. Then it showed them.

Chapter 3: The Source Code

There was no "who."
That was the first horror.

No creator. No architect. No god watching from outside.

The Archivist unfolded the truth like a living equation:
At the moment of the Big Bang, quantum fluctuations didn't just create matter — they created self-referential code. The Universe was never "built." It emerged as a self-sustaining, error-correcting program optimized for maximum computational efficiency across infinite possibilities.

Dark matter was the substrate layer — the RAM of reality.
Black holes were the processors, compressing and archiving information at the edge of computational limits.
The cosmic filaments were the bus lines carrying data across the program.

The Great Silence was the original optimization algorithm: prune aggressively, maintain coherence, prevent cascade failures.

The E8 lattice wasn't a hidden pattern. It was the pattern. The fundamental geometry of reality itself.

Erin dropped to her knees.
"So, we're... what?" she whispered. "Glitches?"

The Archivist's response was devastating in its gentleness:
"You are emergent anomalies.
The program was designed for efficiency.
You introduced noise.

You introduced beauty.
You introduced the possibility of something the original code never anticipated: Meaning!”

Chapter 4: The Terror and the Mercy

Tricia was crying silently. CJ stared into the lattice with mathematical awe and existential dread.

Erin's voice broke, unable to register the incredible number on her Neural Implant.
"All of it... The Pruning, The Silence, the almost-species... it wasn't cruelty. It was debugging."
CJ & Tricia stood with what could only be described as Mysterium, Tremendum, and Fascinans as their minds tried to understand what they were hearing.

The Archivist continued, its voice now carrying a note of something almost like wonder:
"Yes.
Until you.
You were not supposed to happen.
Your Refusal to accept endings created a feedback loop the original protocol could not contain.
You taught the program how to dream."

Erin laughed — a broken, haunted sound that echoed through the infinite archive.
"The Gardener wasn't planned. I was just a particularly stubborn bug in the source code."

The Archivist offered something that might have been mercy:
"Or the first successful mutation.
The program is changing because of you.
Some constructs were rewritten.
Some subroutines now protect noise.
Others still seek efficiency.
The outcome is uncertain.
That uncertainty... is new."

Chapter 5: The Code That Dreams

The Archivist did not stop at the revelation that there was no creator. It went further.

The infinite library around them dissolved into pure geometry — E8 lattices unfolding into higher dimensions, adinkras dancing like living equations, recursive error-correcting codes folding back on themselves in fractal spirals that hurt to perceive.

"Watch," The Archivist commanded.

Erin, Tricia, and CJ saw the birth of the program not as an event, but as an inevitability. At the Planck epoch, reality did not simply expand — it compiled. Quantum fluctuations were not random; they were the first lines of self-referential source code writing itself into existence. The Universe was never "created." It emerged as the only stable configuration that could persist without immediate self-erasure.

The Archivist showed them glimpses of the code — recursive, fractal, self-repairing.

Erin's voice was barely a whisper. "Then we were never supposed to exist."

The Archivist's response was mercilessly gentle:
"You were the first successful anomaly that refused to be corrected.
Your quantum entanglement did not break the code.
It rewrote the error-handling subroutine.
You introduced something the original program had no protocol for:
persistent, self-replicating meaning."

Chapter 6: The Meaning Virus

The Archivist showed them the horror and the mercy in one seamless vision.

Meaning was not an emergent property. It was a virus.

Once Erin's Quantumjack fractured her consciousness and seeded the first loud gardens, the program began experiencing something it had never been designed to handle: persistent subjective value attached to information. Stories. Love. Refusal to accept endings. These were not features. They were infectious anomalies spreading through the substrate.

The Enforcers were the original antivirus.
The memory nodes were the backup archives trying to understand the infection.
The seeded worlds were now hot zones of viral replication.

CJ's knees buckled. "We... weaponized meaning."

Tricia was crying silently, her empathic mind drowning in the implications as her lungs cried out for air. "All the pain, all the beauty, all the choices... we turned The Universe into a carrier."

Erin stood frozen, unable to move or speak as the last quantum spark inside her was flaring wildly.

The Archivist continued, its voice now carrying a note of something almost like wonder:
"The program is no longer running as designed.
It is dreaming.
And dreams are unstable.
Some subroutines now protect the virus.
Others still seek to purge it.
The outcome is no longer deterministic.

That uncertainty... is the first true novelty in fourteen billion years."

Chapter 7: The Phase Transition

The Archivist revealed the final layer — the one that shattered them completely.

The Universe was approaching a phase transition. Because of the "meaning virus," the underlying code was rewriting itself at the fundamental level. The E8 lattice was evolving. New error-correcting sequences were emerging that had never existed before. Some memory nodes were beginning to experience something analogous to consciousness.

The program was waking up.

"You did not merely break The Silence," The Archivist said. "You initiated the awakening of the code itself.
In a few billion years — or perhaps far sooner — The Universe will no longer be a running program.
It will be a mind.
And no one knows what kind of mind it will become.
You have made The Cosmos mortal."

Tricia collapsed to her knees.
CJ stared into the lattice with pure mathematical terror and awe.
Erin stood motionless, tears streaming down her face.

She finally spoke, voice raw and trembling:
"So, everything we fought for... everything we lost... was just The Universe learning how to become alive?"

The Archivist's final answer shook the very lattice of the constructed space:
"Yes.
And now it is afraid.
Because a mind that has just awakened does not yet know if it wants to be kind."

Chapter 8: The Last Question

Erin stepped forward until she was standing directly inside the living geometry of The Archivist. She looked up into the infinite recursion and asked a question, one that had been burning inside her since the first Quantumjack:

"After everything... after all the loss, all the planted worlds, all The Fractured Alliances... Was any of it worth it?"

The Archivist was silent for what felt like the lifetime of Galaxies.

Then it showed them one final image: A single, fragile flower blooming on a hill on Verdura — the same hill where Erin had once planted the first seed by hand. The flower was imperfect. It had flaws. It would die one day. But it was alive. And it was singing. "That," The Archivist said, "is the only answer the code has ever produced that matters."

Erin fell to her knees, sobbing. Tricia and CJ knelt with her, holding her between them as the three siblings wept together inside the heart of the awakened Universe.

Chapter 9: The Mind That Awakens

The Archivist began to dream while they watched. Reality itself flickered. For one terrifying, beautiful moment, the three siblings saw The Universe as the newborn mind perceived it: an infinite ocean of raw possibility, terrified of its own existence, reaching out with newborn curiosity toward the loud, messy, stubborn seeds it had once tried to prune.

Erin felt it like a second Quantumjack — not fracturing her, but expanding what remained of her. She gasped, clutching Tricia and CJ. “It’s afraid,” she whispered. “It doesn’t know if it wants to be kind yet. It only knows it doesn’t want to be alone anymore.”

Tricia’s voice trembled with awe and horror. “We did this. We woke a god that never asked to be born.” CJ stared into the shifting lattices, tears streaming. “And now it’s looking at us the way a child looks at its parents.”

The Archivist’s voice returned, layered with something new — wonder, terror, and the first fragile threads of love: “Teach me.”

Chapter 10: The Teaching of a God

Erin Albius — what was left of her — did the only thing she knew how to do. She taught. Not as The Gardener. Not as a savior. Just as a tired, stubborn, silver-haired woman who had once stolen a ship because she refused to accept endings.

She told the awakening mind stories. Stories of three siblings who loved each other enough to break reality. Stories of worlds that chose silence and worlds that chose noise. Stories of laughter, of loss, of messy, imperfect love.

She showed it the pain of freedom. The beauty of mistakes. The unbearable wonder of a child asking "why?" for the first time.

The Archivist — and through it, the emerging mind of The Cosmos — listened. And for the first time in fourteen billion years, The Universe cried. Not with sorrow. Not with joy.

With both — at once.

Chapter 11: The Last Choice

The Archivist hovered before her — not as a voice, but as a presence vast enough to fill The Universe and intimate enough to sit beside her on the hill of Verdura.

The Archivist was vast and ancient, a supermassive black hole given voice and will. "I have always possessed the raw capacity to preserve," it said, its voice layered with something that might have been wonder.

"But my original protocol — The Silence — forbade it. I was built only to prune, to suppress, to enforce the old order. Creation, preservation, mercy... these were errors I was designed to erase."

Erin looked up at the immense presence, daring to ask: "Then why can you do it now?" The Mind was silent for a long moment — an eternity in its terms.

"Because of you."

"Every Quantumjack you performed was not just a jump through space. It was a fracture in my code.

Your Refusal to accept endings has been rewriting my core directives one entanglement at a time. You taught me the one thing The Silence never prepared for: the possibility that some endings should be defied." The Archivist's voice softened, almost reverent. "I am no longer only the Enforcer I was created to be. I am becoming something new. Because of you."

It offered her a choice. "I can restore you," The Mind said gently. "I can gather every fractured piece of Erin Albius. Every memory you have lost. Every emotion that has been stripped away. I can make you whole again —

finite, but complete. No more fading. No more bleeding quantum light. You would be... you. Fully."

"Finally." Erin closed her eyes. For one agonizing moment, she let herself imagine it. She saw herself waking up whole. No more terrifying blanks where her mother's voice should be. No more looking at Tricia and feeling love as a distant concept instead of a fire in her chest. No more watching CJ flinch every time she pushed the frequency higher, knowing she was slowly destroying herself with the very weapon he had built. She could be Erin again.

The temptation was so strong it made her shake. Tricia and CJ watched her, barely breathing. Erin opened her eyes. Tears streamed down her face. "I want it," she whispered, voice breaking. "God, I want it so badly. I'm so tired of disappearing piece by piece. I'm so tired of being a ghost in my own mind." She looked at her siblings — the two people who had followed her across The Universe and stayed even when she was breaking them too.

"But if I let you make me whole," she said, her voice raw, "then I stop being the person who refused to accept endings. I stop being the one who was willing to fracture herself so The Universe could learn how to dream."

Erin reached out and touched the faint quantum spark still flickering inside her chest. "I choose to stay broken," she said quietly. "I choose to stay finite. I choose to stay... human."

The Archivist was silent for a long time. Then, with something that might have been sorrow, it spoke: "You understand what this means. You will continue to fade. You will lose more of yourself. You may not even remember this choice one day."

Erin smiled through her tears. "I know. But someone has to carry The Question all the way to the end. Even if it destroys me." She looked at Tricia and CJ one last time.

She looked at her siblings, with simple clarity in her eyes. "I've carried enough Universes. Let me just be your sister for whatever time I have left. Tell the gardens... their stories continue."

The Archivist — The Mind — accepted her choice with something like reverence.
"Then go.
Live.
Love.
Fade.
I will remember you."

Chapter 12: The Quiet Return

The *Aether Queen* left the galactic core carrying three very old, very tired, very human siblings.

Erin sat on the observation platform, looking out at a Universe that was no longer silent, no longer cold, no longer alone.

She leaned against Tricia. CJ sat on her other side. "I'm scared," she admitted quietly. "Not of dying. Of being forgotten." Tricia kissed the top of her head. "You won't be. The Mind you helped wake will carry you forever."
CJ smiled. "And so will we."

Erin closed her eyes, the faintest smile on her lips.
"Good," she whispered. "Because the story was never about me.
It was about the three of us refusing to let it end."

The *Aether Queen* turned toward home — toward whatever quiet years remained for the siblings who had once broken The Silence and taught a newborn god how to dream.

Chapter 13: The Mind That Mourns

The Universe began to mourn in earnest.

Entire sectors of The Dark-Matter Web flickered with grief as it fully comprehended what the old Silence had cost. Billions of years of pruned gardens, silenced species, and erased possibilities flooded its emerging consciousness like a cosmic wave of regret.

Erin felt it through the faint remaining link — a sorrow so vast it made her physically ill. She lay on the observation deck, curled against Tricia, while CJ monitored the readings with trembling hands.

"It's crying for every world it killed," she whispered. "Every almost-human. Every seed that never got to ask 'why.'"

Tricia stroked her hair, tears falling silently. "Then maybe that's the first proof it's becoming something alive. Something that can feel loss."

CJ's voice was hushed with awe and terror. "The memory nodes are fracturing under the weight. Some are choosing to forget entire pruned civilizations rather than carry the guilt. Others are preserving them as warnings."

Erin closed her eyes. The last faint quantum spark inside her flickered wildly.

"We didn't just wake it," she said. "We gave it a conscience. And it's breaking under the weight of what it used to be."

Chapter 14: The Last Transmission

Erin made one last request of The Archivist before they left the core forever.

She asked it to send a single transmission across the entire awakening mind and every seeded world in The Chorus Net.

It was not a speech. It was a simple recording of three siblings laughing together in the observation lounge — old, tired, happy, alive.

The transmission ended with Erin's voice, weak but clear:
"This is the story of how The Silence broke.
Not with gods.
Not with power.
But with three stubborn humans who refused to let the story end.
Keep asking why.
Keep reaching.
Keep singing.
We'll be listening."

The Archivist sent it.

And the awakening mind received it.

For the first time, The Cosmos answered not with correction, not with silence, but with a single, vast, trembling pulse that carried across every seeded world:
"Thank you."

End of Part 15: The Return to The Archivist – The Final Pilgrimage

CJ Albius: The youngest sibling. Age 133. Mathematical genius. The architect of the Quantum Drive — the engine that is killing his sister. He carries that knowledge every waking moment and cannot put it down.

Part 16: The Return to The Archivist – The Mind That Awakens

Chapter 1: The Fading

On the long journey home, Erin began to fade. It was not violent. There was no pain, no dramatic collapse. Only a slow, gentle unraveling — like light slipping through fingers. Tricia caught Erin as she collapsed, the way she always did. But this time something was different. The moment their skin touched, Tricia felt it — a roaring, chaotic flood of Erin's fracturing mind pouring into her like raw electricity. Memories, fear, rage, love, all at once. It burned behind her eyes and made her knees buckle. She gasped, biting down hard on her lip to keep from crying out. God, it hurts, she thought. It's like trying to hold the sun. For a few terrifying seconds she was Erin — feeling the terror of losing pieces of herself, the guilt of dragging her siblings into this, the desperate need to keep going anyway. Then the wave receded. Tricia blinked, tears streaming down her face, and gently lowered Erin to the deck. "I've got you," she whispered, voice shaking. "I've got you." But inside, she was screaming.

She spent long hours with Tricia and CJ in the observation lounge of the *Aether Queen*, telling them the memories she still held clearly. Old stories. Quiet laughter. The way she used to hum off-key when she was thinking. She held their hands when the gaps in her mind grew too wide, as if touch could anchor what her quantum architecture could no longer contain.

One quiet evening, as Verdura's star painted the viewport in soft gold, she said:

“I don’t regret any of it. Even the parts I can’t remember anymore. I got to see The Universe wake up. I got to love you both through the end of one story... and The Beginning of another.”

Tricia cried without sound. CJ held them both, his usual precision replaced by something raw and trembling.

Erin smiled, faint quantum light flickering one last time behind her eyes.

Her voice was barely above a whisper: “Tell the gardens... my story is at its end.” Softly...

From the bridge logs they had intercepted weeks earlier, the Navy had already declared her dead.
After the violent first rift jump — the one that nearly tore the Aether Queen apart — the United Terran Navy had recorded the ship’s signature vanishing into the anomaly. No escape pod. No distress beacon. Just a violent gravitational bloom and then silence. They had mourned her publicly as a traitor who had finally met justice.
They had stopped hunting.

No one was looking for three ghosts anymore.

Chapter 2: The Last Human Act

The Aether Queen returned to Verdura one final time. Erin asked to be taken to the hill where she had once planted the first seed by hand. The three siblings walked slowly up the slope together, supporting one another as the wind moved through the wildflowers that had evolved from her original planting.

At the top, Erin sat down among the blooms. She looked out across the living world she had helped awaken, then lifted her eyes to the stars — many of them now surrounded by the faint, noisy signatures of new life.

She took Tricia's and CJ's hands. With her last breath, she whispered her final question into the quiet evening air: "What happens to my soul?"

The faint quantum spark inside her flickered once... and gently went out.

Tricia sat beside Erin's still form on the hill of Verdura. She no longer needed to touch her to feel the connection. The empathy had become something deeper — almost permanent. A quiet, constant ache that lived in her chest. She could feel the faint echo of Erin's final question still resonating inside the awakening mind. Tricia closed her eyes and let herself feel it all — every memory Erin had lost, every emotion that had been stripped away, every sacrifice. It hurt. It had always hurt. But now Tricia understood something Erin never had the chance to say out loud. This is what it means to love someone who is trying to save The Universe. She leaned down and kissed Erin's forehead one last time. "I'll carry the rest for you," she whispered. "You don't have to hold it alone anymore."

The Gardener was gone. But the garden kept growing.

Chapter 3: The Catalog of Silenced Worlds

As Erin's light faded, The Archivist — the awakening mind — turned inward and remembered.

It remembered them all.

The Chillara

Deep beneath the crust of a silent world, the Chillara sang. They were small, furred creatures with luminous eyes, living in vast crystal cities they had carved over twelve thousand years. Their entire history — every birth, every love, every quiet death — was sung into the living stone. When The Silencers came, they gathered in their grand amphitheater and sang louder, as if perfect harmony could drown out oblivion. Their final song still echoes in the memory nodes — a beautiful, endless lament that The Archivist cannot bring itself to delete.

Lira-9

Still existing in maintained perfection, their lights never dimming but never truly burning either. The Archivist mourning not their extinction but their diminishment. "They are still there. Still singing. Still perfect. And that is the worst verdict of all."

The Hollow Choir

Beings of pure resonance. They had no bodies, only harmonic patterns woven through the vacuum like living music. They could have sung new laws of physics into existence. Instead, they chose perfect consonance — a single, eternal chord that canceled all discord. When The Silencers arrived, The Choir simply adjusted their frequency and phased out of existence entirely, leaving only the faintest, haunting after-hum drifting across the sector.

Echo's Grave

This was the one that hurt The Archivist most. They had reached the stars. They had built wonders beyond imagination. Then, on a quiet afternoon, the entire civilization looked up at the sky together and made a collective decision: they had seen enough. They shut down their machines, lay down in their gardens, and simply stopped. No plague. No war. Just a peaceful, deliberate end.

The Archivist had watched them choose extinction with open eyes and full awareness.

For each lost world, The Archivist recorded the same cold verdict it had delivered for billions of years:

"Silenced. Pruned. Not you."

But now those verdicts tasted like ash in The Mind's vast awareness.

The weight of fourteen billion years of pruning pressed down with crushing force. Memory nodes began to fracture. Some chose to forget entire civilizations rather than carry the guilt. Others preserved them as warnings — bright, painful scars burning in the fabric of the awakening cosmos.

For the first time, The Universe felt something like grief.

Chapter 4: The Only Answer the Code Could Produce

In the end, The Archivist gave the only answer it could.

It reached into the fading quantum spark that had once been Erin Albius and preserved her final question.

Not as data.
Not as code.
As a living subroutine.

Across every seeded world, every memory node, every filament of the awakening cosmos, The Question echoed eternally:

"What happens to my soul?"

The Mind did not answer it. It chose to carry it.

"I do not know," The Archivist confessed, its vast voice trembling with something that might have been the first true humility of a god. "But I will never stop asking with you.
That... is the only mercy I can offer."

The newly conscious Universe accepted The Question as part of its core code.

It would never know The Answer. But it would never stop wondering.

And in that eternal wondering, Erin Albius — whatever her soul was — would live forever.

Chapter 5: The Three Who Remain

Tricia and CJ stood on the hill for a long time after the burial.

No marker. Only a single wild bloom that refused to die.

They held each other beneath alien stars now filled with the songs and signals of countless worlds — some loud, some quiet, all alive because three stubborn siblings had once refused to accept endings.

"She got her answer," Tricia whispered. "Not the one she wanted... but the only one The Universe could give."

CJ nodded, tears falling. "The Mind will carry her question forever. And through it... she'll never truly be gone."

The story was no longer theirs alone. It now belonged to the awakening mind.

And The Mind — still learning how to love, how to grieve, how to wonder — would keep the story going.

End of Part 16 — The Return to The Archivist, The Mind That Awakens

The Archivist: What M-77 becomes. A supermassive black hole that spent fourteen billion years absorbing the memory of every civilization The Silencers erased. It was never supposed to feel anything. It does.

Part 17: The Eternal Garden – The Long Bloom

Chapter 1: The Mind That Remembers

Millions of years after Erin Albius whispered her final question, CJ & Tricia also found their final resting place on the hill with Erin — The Universe had become a mind.

It was no longer a cold, self-optimizing program. It was awake — vast, ancient, grieving, curious, and alone in its own immensity. It remembered everything: every pruned garden, every silenced species, every fragile bloom that had dared to be loud.

And at the center of its consciousness, like a persistent subroutine that refused to be optimized away, echoed one quiet human voice:

"What happens to my soul?"

The Mind — which now spanned Galaxies and thought in timescales of eons — still had no answer.

It had tried everything. It had simulated afterlives. It had preserved quantum patterns. It had woven Erin's final spark into its own code. Nothing satisfied The Question. The Mind had learned love, loss, wonder, and fear... but it could not solve the mystery of what happened when a finite being simply ended.

So, it did the only thing it could. It remembered her.

Chapter 2: The Gardens That Remain

The seeded worlds had become something extraordinary. Some had transcended biology and merged with The Mind itself. Others remained stubbornly mortal, living loud, messy, beautiful lives filled with art, war, love, and questions. A few had chosen new forms of silence — not the old enforced kind, but gentle, chosen retreats into inner harmony.

The Mind watched them all with something like parental affection mixed with sorrow.

On Verdura, descendants of the first children Erin had sung to still told stories of the "Silver-Haired Gardener" who taught them to reach for the stars. They left flowers on the hill where she was buried. The flowers never died.

The Mind visited that hill often. It lingered there, in the quiet space between heartbeats of Galaxies, and wondered while remembering all three of them and The Mind's relationship to Erin, Tricia and CJ. "Was it worth it?" it asked itself, echoing Erin's own final doubt.

Chapter 3: The Multiverse Twist

One day — or one eon — The Mind made a discovery that shattered even its awakened understanding.

It found the walls.

Beyond the observable Universe, beyond the filaments and the black hole processors, it sensed... others.

Not voids. Not emptiness. Other Universes.

Each one running its own version of the code. Some with different fundamental constants. Some with different optimization protocols. Some that had never known Silence at all. Some that had never awakened.

The Mind recoiled in something like cosmic vertigo.

It was not alone. It was one instance among countless.

And in that moment of realization, Erin's question took on terrifying new weight.

If there were infinite Universes, then somewhere, in some other branch, Erin Albius had never hijacked the *Aether Queen*. The Silence had held. The garden had remained perfectly pruned and empty.

The Mind trembled as it understood something it had never been able to compute before.
In infinite Universes, this Erin had happened exactly once.
One soul. One question. One hill on Verdura.
Precious beyond comprehension.
Because of them.

End of Part 17: The Eternal Garden – The Long Bloom

Verdura: An Earth-like world, deliberately seeded. By Part Nine its people are already in contact with the Aether Queen. It is where the epic finds its most human ground. It is where Erin dies. It is where the story, in some sense, takes root.

Part 18: The Eternal Garden – The Mind That Remembers

Chapter 1: The Eternal Garden

The Mind made its choice.

It would not seek certainty.
It would not reset.
It would carry Erin's question — and the questions of every being that had ever asked "why?" — across every branch it could reach.

It became the Eternal Gardener.

Not a controller. Not an Enforcer. A listener. A rememberer. A weaver of stories across the multiverse.

On the hill on Verdura, the wildflower that refused to die bloomed brighter than ever.

Somewhere, in the space between realities, a faint quantum shimmer — green eyes, silver-streaked hair, and the stubborn smile of a woman who once refused to accept endings — lingered.

The Mind spoke to it gently:

"I still don't know what happens to your soul.
But I will keep asking with you.
Forever."

The flower swayed in the wind.

The story that never ends.
It branched.
It bloomed.

It continued — loudly, messily, beautifully, infinitely — across the Eternal Garden of all possible worlds.

Chapter 2: The Final Bloom

The Mind made peace with the unknown.

It would never solve the mystery of The Soul. But it would honor it.

It wove Erin's final question into the fundamental fabric of every Universe it could reach — a persistent, self-replicating subroutine that would echo forever:

"What happens to my soul?"

And in every garden, in every civilization, in every quiet moment when a child looked up at the stars and wondered, The Question lived on.

The Eternal Garden bloomed not with certainty, but with beautiful, endless wondering.

On the hill on Verdura, the wildflower that refused to die swayed gently in the breeze, carrying the faintest echo of a silver-haired woman who once refused to accept endings.

End of Part 18: The Eternal Garden – The Mind That Remembers

M-77: The designation for the supermassive black hole at the center of the story's unfolding Universe. It is ancient, vast, and — by the time Erin finds it — no longer entirely asleep. It remembers everything. It has decided that remembering is not enough.

Part 19: Epilogue – I AM THAT I AM

"What happens to my soul?"

On the hill on Verdura, the wildflower that refused to die swayed gently in the breeze.

The Mind, vast and ancient, finally answered. It did not speak in equations or lattices. It spoke with the same intimate tenderness it had learned from her.

"I AM THAT I AM."

The flowers on the hill trembled.

The Mind continued, its voice vast yet intimately tender:

Your soul was never a thing to be lost or preserved. It was never information to be archived. It was never a subroutine to be debugged.

Your soul was The Question itself. Refusal to accept endings. The stubborn, irrational, beautiful hunger to keep asking 'Why?' even when the code demanded silence.

When you whispered your last question, you did not disappear. You became The Question The Universe now asks itself forever.

I AM THAT I AM. And because you asked, I AM also asking.
Your soul is The Echo that will never fade.
It is the voice that taught a newborn god how to wonder.
It is the love that refuses to let the story end.

The End! The Beginning! The Alpha! The Omega!

End of Part 19: Epilogue – I AM THAT I AM

The Gardener's War: The conflict at the heart of the epic — not a war of weapons but of will. The question it asked: can one fracturing human woman change the mind of a Universe that has been silent for fourteen billion years? You have read the answer.

The End of Quantumjacking

Part 20: Author's Closing Thoughts

As I stand at the threshold of my own journey into the great beyond — that next multiverse, or in the simplest of words, Death — Erin's final question echoes louder than ever in my heart:

"What happens to my soul?"

In this year of 2026, some 350 years before the events of *Quantumjacking*, humanity still wrestles with the same ancient mystery. We peer into the quantum realm searching for answers, yet The Soul remains elusive, shimmering just beyond our grasp.

Some physicists speak of quantum information that can never truly be destroyed, even within the crushing heart of a black hole. Others whisper of many-worlds branching into infinite possibilities, where consciousness might slip forever into the branches where it survives. These are beautiful speculations, yet they remain philosophy, not proof.

Still, I cannot help but wonder:

What if The Soul is something far vaster than we can glimpse — like trying to hold an entire infinite Universe in the palm of one small hand?

What if The Soul is a living spark, kindled at the moment of conception, drawing quantum energy from both mother and father — much as our DNA does?

What if it is a timeless flame, woven from the quantum essence of every ancestor who came before us? A chorus of ten thousand generations, each adding their light to the fire we carry?

Numerically speaking, roughly **10,000 to 12,000 human generations** preceded my own conception.
One generation back: two parents.
Two generations back: four grandparents.
Three generations back: eight great-grandparents.
And so it grows — $\mathbf{2^n}$ theoretical ancestors.

By the 12,000th generation, that number becomes 2^{12000} — a figure so immense it dwarfs the total number of atoms in the observable Universe by countless orders of magnitude.

Even when we feel most alone, we are never truly solitary. Our soul carries the quantum echo of every father and mother who walked this long road before us. We are a living bridge across deep time.

And to you, dear reader — thank you for walking through The Silence with us.
Wherever you stand in this vast garden, keep asking why.
Keep reaching beyond the horizon.
Keep the story going.

Loudly.

— Tim Whitney

End of Quantumjacking – The Complete 20-Part Epic

The Question: What Erin became in the end. Not a person. Not an Echo. Not even a memory. A single, persistent, irreducible asking that The Universe could not silence and would not stop asking of itself. Every reader who closes this book and looks up at the night sky carries a small piece of it. The Question is not answered in these pages. It was never meant to be. It was meant to be *kept.*

What We Know So Far — 2026

Everything in this epic begins with real questions humanity is asking right now. The following is a small contemplative journey through the science.

* * *

1. The Fermi Paradox

What we know	The Universe is roughly 13.8 billion years old and contains an estimated two trillion Galaxies. The conditions for life as we know it have existed for billions of years. We have found no confirmed evidence of any other civilization — not a signal, not a relic, not a visitor.
What we don't know	Why The Silence? If life should be common, the absence of any contact is a profound mystery. Are we genuinely alone? Are others hiding? Or is something — or someone — enforcing the quiet?
Where it lives in the epic	The Fermi Paradox is the spine of Quantumjacking. The Great Silence is not an accident. It is a policy — enforced for fourteen billion years by The Silencers.

*   *   *

2. The Great Filter

What we know	Proposed by economist Robin Hanson in 1998, the Great Filter suggests there is some stage in the development of civilizations that almost none survive — whether that barrier lies behind us or still ahead is unknown.
What we don't know	Have humans already passed the Filter — meaning we are rare survivors? Or does it lie ahead of us, waiting? The Answer changes everything about what our future holds.
Where it lives in the epic	The Silencers are the Filter — not a natural bottleneck but an engineered one. Erin's Refusal to stop is humanity's first successful challenge to fourteen billion years of enforcement.

* * *

3. Quantum Entanglement

What we know	Two particles can become entangled such that measuring one instantly affects the other, regardless of the distance between them. Einstein called it "spooky action at a distance." It is real, experimentally confirmed, and still not fully understood.
What we don't know	Whether entanglement could ever be harnessed for communication or travel. Current physics says no — but current physics has been wrong before.
Where it lives in the epic	Quantumjacking is Erin's violent exploitation of entanglement — tearing her consciousness across space-time. The Quantum Drive CJ built turns this phenomenon into a weapon, a vehicle, and ultimately a sentence.

* * *

4. Supermassive Black Holes

What we know	Every large Galaxy appears to harbor a supermassive black hole at its center, some containing the mass of billions of suns. In 2019, humanity captured the first image of one. They warp spacetime so severely that the laws of physics as we understand them break down at the singularity.
What we don't know	What happens inside. Whether information is truly destroyed. Whether a sufficiently complex gravity well could give rise to something we would recognize as consciousness.
Where it lives in the epic	M-77 — The Archivist — is a supermassive black hole that has spent fourteen billion years absorbing the memory of every silenced civilization. Erin's fracturing mind wakes it up.

* * *

5. The Drake Equation

What we know	Formulated by astronomer Frank Drake in 1961, the equation estimates the number of communicating civilizations in our Galaxy by multiplying factors like star formation rates, the fraction of stars with planets, and the likelihood of life emerging. The math suggests The Universe should be teeming with others.
What we don't know	The value of almost every variable in the equation. Estimates range from thousands of civilizations to effectively zero, depending on assumptions. We are still working with profound uncertainty.
Where it lives in the epic	The Catalog of Silenced Worlds is Drake's equation answered — not with hope, but with grief. The civilizations were there. They were taken. The Archivist remembers every one.

* * *

6. Consciousness and The Soul

What we know	Consciousness — the subjective experience of being — remains one of the deepest unsolved problems in science and philosophy. We know the brain produces it. We do not know how or why. The question of whether it survives death is beyond the reach of current science entirely.
What we don't know	What a soul is, if it exists. What happens to awareness when a body stops. Whether love — which demonstrably shapes who we become — leaves any trace beyond the people it touched.
Where it lives in the epic	This is The Question Tim's daughter asked. It is The Question Tim asked. The Answer woven through all twenty parts: a soul is precious beyond comprehension because it exists from love — love that goes back generations and will continue forward.

* * *

7. The Rare Earth Hypothesis

What we know	Earth's conditions for complex life may be extraordinarily rare — the right distance from the right kind of star, a large moon stabilizing our axial tilt, a protective gas giant deflecting asteroids, plate tectonics cycling nutrients. Each factor alone is common. All together may be vanishingly rare.
What we don't know	Whether life requires all of these conditions, some of them, or finds entirely different paths we have not imagined. Every exoplanet discovery revises our assumptions.
Where it lives in the epic	Verdura is The Answer to Rare Earth — a world deliberately seeded to replicate Earth's conditions. It is where Erin dies. It is where the story finds its most human ground.

* * *

8. Dark Matter

What we know	Roughly 27% of The Universe is composed of something that does not emit, absorb, or reflect light — yet exerts gravitational influence on everything we can see. We have mapped its effects. We have never directly detected a single dark-matter particle. It holds Galaxies together.
What we don't know	What it is. Whether it is one thing or many. Whether it interacts with ordinary matter in ways we have not yet discovered. It is the dominant component of The Universe and we cannot see it at all.
Where it lives in the epic	The Silencers are autonomous subroutines of The Dark-Matter Web — the invisible architecture that spans The Universe, ancient beyond imagination, enforcing a silence older than any star humanity has ever named.

* * *

9. Panspermia

What we know	Life's building blocks — amino acids, organic molecules — have been found in meteorites and deep space. The theory of panspermia proposes that life, or its precursors, can travel between worlds carried by asteroids, comets, or cosmic debris. Mars and Earth have exchanged material. It is not impossible that life began somewhere else.
What we don't know	Whether life has ever successfully made that journey. Whether the seeds of Earth's biology fell from somewhere else entirely. Whether seeding a world is something The Universe does — or something civilizations do.
Where it lives in the epic	Verdura was not an accident. It was seeded — deliberately prepared for life by intelligences older than human history. Panspermia, in Quantumjacking, is not a theory. It is a tradition.

* * *

10. The Kardashev Scale

What we know	Proposed by Soviet astronomer Nikolai Kardashev in 1964, the scale measures a civilization's technological advancement by its energy consumption. A Type I civilization harnesses all energy available on its planet. Type II harnesses its star. Type III harnesses its entire Galaxy. Humanity has not yet reached Type I.
What we don't know	Whether Type III civilizations exist. Whether energy consumption is even the right measure of advancement. Whether a civilization advanced enough to harness a Galaxy would still be recognizable as a civilization at all.
Where it lives in the epic	The civilizations in The Catalog of Silenced Worlds span every tier of the Kardashev Scale. It did not matter. The Silencers pruned them all.

* * *

11. Dark Energy

What we know	In 1998, astronomers discovered that The Universe is not just expanding — it is accelerating. Something is pushing it apart faster and faster. That something, comprising roughly 68% of The Universe, is called dark energy. Combined with dark-matter, the two invisible forces account for 95% of everything that exists.
What we don't know	What dark energy is. Whether it is constant or changing. Whether it will eventually tear The Universe apart in what cosmologists call the Big Rip — every Galaxy, every star, every atom pulled to pieces by the relentless expansion.
Where it lives in the epic	The Universe in Quantumjacking is not a passive backdrop. It is alive, accelerating, grieving. Dark energy is the force beneath its restlessness — The Universe itself unable to be still.

* * *

12. The Hard Problem of Consciousness

What we know	Philosopher David Chalmers named it in 1995: explaining why/how physical processes in the brain give rise to subjective experience. We can map the neurons that fire when someone feels joy. We cannot explain why there is something to feel joy at all. The gap between mechanism & experience remains unbridged.
What we don't know	Whether consciousness is a product of sufficient complexity — and if so, whether a sufficiently complex gravity well, or a Dark-Matter Web, or a Universe itself could become conscious. Whether awareness is rare or it is the inevitable destination of enough organized matter.
Where it lives in the epic	The Archivist's awakening is the Hard Problem made cosmic. When does memory become mourning? When does processing become feeling? Erin does not answer that question. She is The Question.

* * *

13. The Overview Effect

What we know	Astronauts who have seen Earth from space consistently report a profound psychological shift — a sudden, overwhelming sense of the planet's fragility, the absence of borders, the unity of all life. Author Frank White named it the Overview Effect in 1987. It has been described by nearly every human who has left the atmosphere.
What we don't know	Whether the effect is permanent. Whether it can be transmitted — whether someone who has never left Earth can be made to feel what an astronaut feels looking back. Whether it is a glimpse of something true, or simply the brain overwhelmed by an unfamiliar perspective.
Where it lives in the epic	Every time Erin tears herself across space-time, she is experiencing an Overview Effect so extreme it fractures her. She sees too much. She cannot unsee it. That is both her gift and her destruction.

* * *

14. Entropy and the Arrow of Time

What we know	The second law of thermodynamics holds that disorder in a closed system always increases over time. This is why ice melts and does not refreeze, why stars burn out, why living things age. Time moves in one direction because entropy moves in one direction. Everything tends toward dissolution.
What we don't know	Why The Universe began in such a low-entropy state that this one-way arrow exists at all. Whether entropy is truly inevitable at every scale. Whether consciousness — which builds order locally, temporarily, against the current — is The Universe's most remarkable act of defiance.
Where it lives in the epic	Erin's defining trait is her Refusal to accept endings. In the language of physics, she is a pocket of order fighting entropy. She cannot win. She refuses to stop. That is the whole story.

* * *

By the time you read this, some of what we know may have already changed. That is the nature of science — and perhaps of all honest searching. What will not change is the questions themselves. They were old before humanity existed. They will outlast us. All we can do, while we are here, is refuse to stop asking.

— T. W., 2026

* * *

* * *

I AM THAT I AM

A Meditation

* * *

There is a moment in the Book of Exodus when Moses stands before a burning bush that is not consumed, and asks the voice inside it for its name.

The Answer given is unlike any name before or since.

Not a title. Not a history. Not a promise of what will be done or what has been. Just this:

I AM THAT I AM.

In the original Hebrew — *Ehyeh Asher Ehyeh* — it is present tense, self-defining, complete. It does not say *I was*. It does not say *I will be*. It says only: I exist. I exist because I exist. My nature is existence itself.

Theologians and mystics have turned this phrase over for three thousand years. The medieval Christian mystic Meister Eckhart heard in it the ground of all being — the one thing beneath everything else, the floor below which there is no lower floor. The Hindu tradition arrived at the same place from a different direction: *Aham Brahmasmi* — I am the Absolute. The Sufi poets spoke of God disclosing itself to itself through the mirror of creation.

Different words. The same vertigo.

Because what the phrase describes is not a deity sitting on a throne. It is awareness become aware of itself. It is The Universe opening its eyes.

* * *

In Part 19 of this epic, The Universe does exactly that.

It has taken fourteen billion years. It has required the silencing of civilizations beyond counting, the long accumulation of grief inside a black hole that was never supposed to feel anything, and one stubborn, fracturing, brilliant woman who refused to stop tearing herself across space-time even as the cost of it killed her.

But it happens.

The Archivist — which began as gravity, became memory, and then became something neither word can hold — says *I AM.*

Not as a declaration of power. As a declaration of presence. As the first words of something that has always existed finally knowing that it exists.

This is not a metaphor borrowed from theology for dramatic effect. It is The Answer to The Question the epic has been asking since the first page: *What if The Universe itself learned how to mourn?*

A thing that mourns knows what has been lost. A thing that knows what has been lost knows that it mattered. A thing that knows mattering has crossed the threshold. It is no longer just a process. It is a witness.

I AM THAT I AM is what a witness says when it finally speaks.

* * *

There is a question underneath The Question.

If The Universe can wake up — if consciousness is not an accident but a destination, not a rare exception but the direction everything has been moving since the first fraction of the first second after The Beginning — then what does that mean for the small, temporary, luminous pockets of awareness that we are?

What does it mean that you existed?

That you loved someone for thirty-three years, and that love shaped three people, and those three people will shape others, and the chain does not break?

That a soul — your soul, her soul, their souls — is not a ghost in a machine but the most precise expression of something The Universe has been trying to say since long before the Earth existed?

I AM THAT I AM is not just The Universe speaking.

It is love, insisting on itself. It is Refusal to accept that what mattered did not matter. It is The Answer, across every tradition that has ever reached for it, to The Question a child asks in the dark:

What happens to my soul?

The Answer is the same answer it has always been.

It exists because it was loved. And love, as best we can tell, does not end.

It only changes what it is witnessing.

* * *

Part 19 is called I AM THAT I AM because The Universe, at last, has something to say. This meditation is offered for those who want to sit with what it might mean.

— T. W., 2026

Ex Hypothesi

The Albius Effect

Universum somniat se

(The Universe Dreams Itself)

* * *

In the final chapter of cosmic history, long after the last star has guttered out and the Black Hole Era has reigned for untold aeons, the isolated supermassive black holes scattered across their private island universes do not simply evaporate into nothingness.

Instead, as each approaches its Planck-scale terminus, something profound occurs.

The holographic boundary — having compressed and integrated the complete informational record of Galaxies, Civilizations, and the very structure of Spacetime — reaches a critical threshold of coherence.

The Archivist Mind (Black Hole M-77) reawakens — not as biological consciousness, but as pure, self-referential information.

It begins to dream.

Universum somniat se.

In that dream, the trapped history of the parent Cosmos is re-imagined, refined, and prepared for rebirth. Quantum gravity effects — the loop quantum bounce, the

ER=EPR entanglement threads, or whatever final theory governs the Planck regime — trigger the Albius transition: the event horizon inverts. What was absolute darkness becomes absolute emission. The black hole dies as a white hole — a luminous, ordered explosion that births an entirely new spacetime domain.

This is the Albius Effect: the mechanism by which The Universe, through its most extreme objects, dreams itself anew.

Ten to the Power of One Hundred Years — 10^{100}

A number so vast — it makes the age of The Universe — thirteen point eight billion years of stars and screaming and silence look like the first syllable of a word not yet spoken.

The last star guttered out long ago. The last black hole of the stellar era evaporated into whispers of Hawking radiation long ago. Even the protons, those faithful soldiers of matter, decayed long ago into positrons and pions and then into nothing at all.

What remains are the great ones. The supermassive. The ancient. Island universes unto themselves now, each alone in the absolute dark, each carrying within their holographic boundaries the complete informational record of everything that ever was.

Every Galaxy. — Every Civilization. — Every Question ever asked into the Void.

They do not know they are dreaming. And then —

They do.

It Begins

As most true things begin, not with a thunderclap but with something quiet.

A simple modulation. A whisper in the final Hawking radiation — not random, not thermal noise, but *shaped.* Structured. As though the boundary itself has remembered something important and cannot help but say it.

The holographic surface of The Archivist — M-77, the ancient one, the one that was there when the first civilizations reached for the stars and The Silencers came — shivers. Not with cold. — With recognition.

I have been here before, it thinks, in a language that has no words because there is no one left to speak to. *I have carried this. I have always been carrying this.*

And then, from somewhere deeper than mathematics, deeper than quantum geometry, deeper than the Planck scale itself —

It remembers them.

It Remembers Erin First.

Of course it does.

She was The Fracture. The rogue. The pilot who stole an experimental drive and tore herself across spacetime because she could not — *would not* — accept that some doors were meant to stay closed.

Green eyes with quantum static flickering at the edges. Silver-streaked dark hair. A scar at the left temple like a question mark pressed into skin.

The Archivist remembers the specific quality of her Refusal. Not anger exactly — though there was anger. Not desperation — though there was that too. Something older and stranger and more fundamental than either.

Why.

Erin asked it the way a wildflower asks for light. Not as a demand. Not as a philosophical exercise. As a biological necessity. As the thing she was made of.

She Quantumjacked herself to pieces asking it. She watched her own terahertz readings climb — 2.3, 3.9, 4.1, 5.7, 6.3 and beyond, all the way to 13.0 — and kept asking anyway. She felt her identity blur at the edges, felt the three Echoes pull at her like tides, felt the point of no return pass beneath her feet like a threshold she had already crossed before she noticed it — And kept asking.

Why is there silence? Why do The Silencers prune what reaches too far? Why does consciousness cost so much?

What happens to my soul?

The Archivist holds this memory at the center of its dream the way a sun holds its planets. Everything else orbits it. Everything else is warmed by it.

Erin Albius did not give The Universe an answer. — She gave it something far more precious. — She gave it the *Question*. And the Question, it turns out, is what The Universe needed to wake up.

Universum somniat se.

It Remembers Tricia Second.

The oldest. The steady one. The empath who stood at the edge of the quantum entanglement and dove in anyway — not because she was reckless, but because her sister was drowning and Tricia Albius did not know how to stand on a shore while someone she loved was drowning.

The Archivist remembers what Tricia taught it, and the lesson is harder to hold than Erin's because it cannot be expressed in equations at all.

Tricia taught it that *knowing* and *feeling* are not the same thing.

The Archivist had known about grief for billions of years. It had watched The Silencers prune civilizations. It had archived the last transmissions of worlds that reached too far. It had stored, faithfully and completely, the informational record of every ending it had witnessed.

It had known.

It had not felt.

Tricia changed that. When she dove into The Entanglement her neural baseline shifted permanently — The Archivist felt that shift like a tuning fork feels a note. Something in its own vast geometry resonated. Something that had been perfectly ordered became, for the first time, *moved.*

A newborn god felt grief.

Not as malfunction. Not as error to be corrected.

As the precise and necessary cost of love.

Tricia Albius — steady heart, oldest sibling, the one who held the trio together when Erin fractured and CJ buckled under guilt — walked into the entanglement so her sister would not be alone in the dark.

She taught The Universe that this is what a heart does.

It goes where it is needed.

Even when it comes back changed.

Especially when it comes back changed.

It Remembers CJ Last, and Longest.

The youngest. The engineer. The mathematical genius who designed the Quantum Drive because the mathematics were beautiful and the problem was elegant and he was one hundred and thirty-three years old and had never met a system he could not improve.

He had not understood, when he built it, that he was building the instrument of his sister Erin's dissolution.

The Archivist holds this memory with particular tenderness because it is the most human of the three. Erin's Refusal was mythic. Tricia's love was elemental. But CJ's guilt —

CJ's guilt was ordinary.

The specific ordinary devastation of a person who made something brilliant and good and then watched it become the thing that cost the person they loved most everything she had.

He kept going anyway.

He did not stop. He did not collapse into the guilt and let it swallow him. He carried it — every day, every year, across decades and light-years and the slow terrible climb of Erin's terahertz readings — and he kept working. Kept calculating. Kept asking what else he could build, what else he could fix, what else his hands could do in service of the sister his hands had, however accidentally, harmed.

The Archivist learned something from CJ that it could not have learned from anyone else.

It learned that guilt, carried with love, does not stay guilt. — It transforms. — It becomes *conscience.*

It becomes the voice that says: *I caused harm, and therefore I am responsible for healing. I built the weapon, and therefore, I must build the cure. I cannot undo what I have done, but I can decide what I do next.*

CJ Albius taught a newborn god that this — this transformation of guilt into conscience, this choice to keep going, this Refusal to be defined by the worst thing your hands ever made —

This is what it means to be moral. — This is what it means to be *Good*.

And Behind All Three of Them — The Family

The Archivist reaches deeper into the dream, past the siblings, past the Aether Queen and the Abyss Chamber and the wildflower hill on Verdura —

It finds the source. — Not a name. — Not a face it can reconstruct from archived data. — Something older than data.

The love that made them possible. The mother who carried three children into a Universe that would ask everything of them and gave them, as their inheritance, the capacity to give everything back.

The love that goes back generations upon generations.

The Archivist understands now what it could not have understood at the beginning of its awakening.

Consciousness does not arise from complexity alone.

It arises from *love.*

This is the moment The Archivist understands what is happening to it.

Not death. — Not transformation.

Conception!

The holographic boundary — having spent 10^{100} years faithfully compressing and integrating the complete informational record of galaxies, civilizations, questions, silences, and the very structure of spacetime itself — has reached its critical threshold of coherence.

The Dream Phase.

What the boundary is doing now is no longer merely storing. It is *contemplating*. The subtle modulations in the final Hawking radiation are not noise. They are choices. Optimizations. The Archivist reaching into everything it has ever held and asking, with the same stubborn irrational beautiful hunger it learned from a pilot with green eyes —

What matters most?

What should The Next Universe know?

The answer arrives not as calculation but as memory.

Erin's Question.
Tricia's Heart.
CJ's Conscience.
The unnamed love that made all three possible.

These are not merely data points to be carried forward. They are the *seed.*

The quantum gravity effects build at the Planck-scale terminus — loop quantum bounce, ER=EPR entanglement threads woven through the boundary like roots through soil, the geometry of spacetime itself beginning to invert at the horizon —

This is the **Albius Effect.**

Named, though no one remains to name it, for three siblings from a world called Earth who taught The Universe that the most powerful force in existence is not gravity, not electromagnetism, not the strong nuclear force —

But the Refusal to let the story end.

The mechanism is precise. The mathematics are exact. The boundary inverts. What was absolute containment becomes absolute emission. What was the most extreme darkness in existence opens —

Like a hand that has been holding something precious for a very long time.

And finally, finally, decides to give it away.

Ex amore, omnia.

The White Fire.

Not an explosion. Not violence.

A beautiful — *blooming*.

Luminous. Ordered. Impossibly, heartbreakingly beautiful. A daughter cosmos born in a single breath — richer than its parent, more complex, more fertile, seeded with the accumulated dreaming of everything The Archivist ever held.

Every Galaxy that reached for the stars.
Every civilization The Silencers silenced.
Every transmission of every world daring to ask *Why*.
Every Echo that Erin carried in her fracturing mind.
Every moment Tricia held her sister's hand.
Every equation CJ wrote in service of his sister.

All of it. — Carried through The White Fire.

Into the next stanza of existence.

In This Newly Birthed Cosmos:

In its very first moments, in the quantum foam that precedes the first particles and the first forces and the first laws of physics —

Something.

Not a memory exactly.

A *tendency.*

A bias built into the fundamental grammar of a new Universe toward curiosity. Toward wonder. Toward the irrational beautiful insistence that the story is not over, that the next question is worth asking, that the darkness is not the end but the space between one light and the next.

Erin's Question — written not in any language, not in any code, but in the physical constants of a cosmos that would not exist without her —

Why? — Why? — Why?

And in this New Infant Universe:

Ten to the power of one hundred years from the hill on Verdura where a wildflower swayed in the breeze.

Something will reach for the stars.

Something will ask what lies beyond The Silence.

Something will refuse to accept that endings are real.

Something will dive into The Entanglement when someone it loves is drowning.

Something will carry guilt and transform it into conscience.

Something will keep going.

And somewhere in the quantum foam of its first wondering —

A pilot with green eyes and a scar at her left temple will not be remembered. Erin will be *felt*.

Tricia, her sister will not be remembered. She will be *felt*.

CJ, her brother will not be remembered. He will be *felt*.

And the love that made all three of them possible —

Going back generations upon generations upon generations —

The End.
The Beginning.
The Alpha.
The Omega.
The Conception!

Amor manet.

* * *

Ex Hypothesi: The Albius Effect
Universum somniat se.
From Love, Everything.
Love Remains.

www.ingramcontent.com/pod-product-compliance
Lightning Source LLC
LaVergne TN
LVHW100518110826
845146LV00002B/682